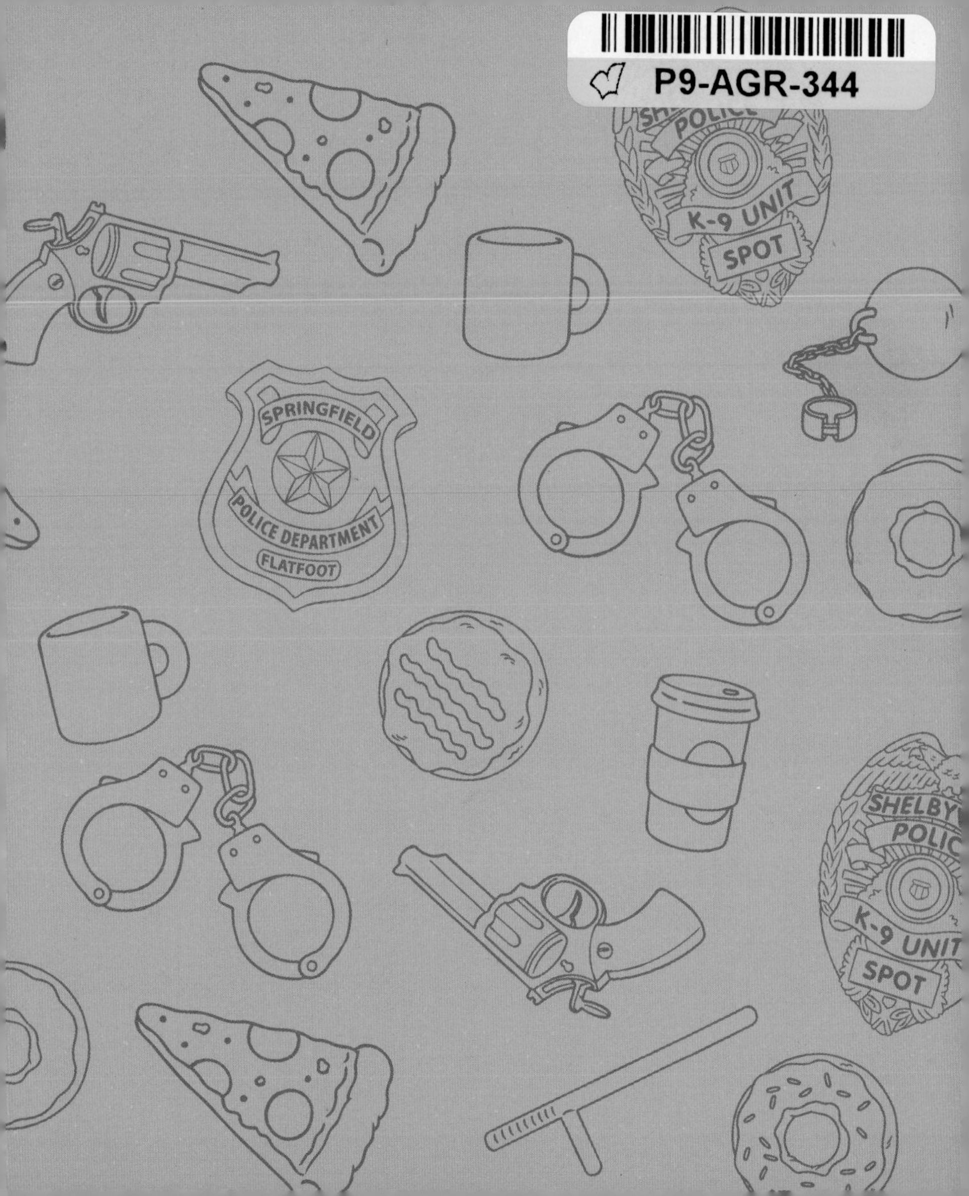
K-9 UNIT
SPOT
SPRINGFIELD
POLICE DEPARTMENT
FLATFOOT
SHELBY
K-9 UNIT
SPOT

CHIEF WIGGUM'S BOOK
OF CRIME AND PUNISHMENT

THE SIMPSONS™ LIBRARY OF WISDOM
CHIEF WIGGUM'S BOOK OF CRIME AND PUNISHMENT

Copyright © 2010 by
Matt Groening Productions, Inc. All rights reserved.

Printed in China

No part of this book may be used or reproduced in any manner whatsoever without written permission
except in the case of brief quotations embodied in critical articles and reviews. For information address
HarperCollins Publishers,
10 East 53rd Street, New York, NY 10022.

FIRST EDITION
ISBN 978-0-06-178743-0

10 11 12 13 14 SC 10 9 8 7 6 5 4 3 2 1

Publisher: Matt Groening
Creative Director: Bill Morrison
Managing Editor: Terry Delegeane
Director of Operations: Robert Zaugh
Art Director: Nathan Kane
Special Projects Art Director: Serban Cristescu
Production Manager: Christopher Ungar
Assistant Art Director: Chia-Hsien Jason Ho
Production/Design: Karen Bates, Nathan Hamill, Art Villanueva
Staff Artist: Mike Rote
Administration: Ruth Waytz, Pete Benson
Legal Guardian: Susan A. Grode

THE SIMPSONS™ LIBRARY OF WISDOM

Edited by Bill Morrison
Book Design, Art Direction, and Production by Serban Cristescu
Contributing Editor: Terry Delegeane

HarperCollins Editors: Hope Innelli and Jeremy Cesarec

Contributing Artists:
KAREN BATES, JOHN COSTANZA, SERBAN CRISTESCU,
DAN DAVIS, MIKE DECARLO, JOHN DELANEY, PETE GOMEZ, ISTVAN MAJOROS,
BILL MORRISON, KIMBERLY NARSETE, KEVIN M. NEWMAN, JOEY NILGES,
MIKE ROTE, ROBERT STANLEY, ERICK TRAN

Contributing Writers:
TONY DIGEROLAMO, SCOTT M. GIMPLE, MARY TRAINOR, PATRICK M. VERRONE

Special Thanks to:
N. Vyolet Diaz, Deanna MacLellan, Helio Salvatierra, Sherri Smith, Mili Smythe, and Ursula Wendel

CHIEF WIGGUM'S BOOK
OF CRIME AND PUNISHMENT

HARPER

NEW YORK • LONDON • TORONTO • SYDNEY

CHIEF WIGGUM'S TOP 40

1. LARD LAD'S DONUT-FILLED DONUTS.
2. ALL-YOU-CAN-EAT PANCAKE BUFFETS.
3. MORNING NAPS IN THE PATROL CAR.
4. LATE-NIGHT NAPS ON STAKEOUTS.
5. AFTERNOON NAPS AT MY DESK.
6. CHINTZY POP SONGS.
7. MONA SIMPSON.
8. HUSH MONEY.
9. BLACKJACKS.
10. KICKBACKS.
11. KNICKKNACKS.
12. PARTY SNACKS.
13. SALT-AND-PEPPER SPRAY.
14. NICKEL-PLATED LEG IRONS.
15. STAINLESS-STEEL HANDCUFFS.
16. TIME-OUT GAS.
17. BLACK CHROME COMBINATION TACTICAL BATON/FLASHLIGHT/BACKSCRATCHERS.
18. MEGAPHONE NIGHT AT THE KARAOKE BAR.

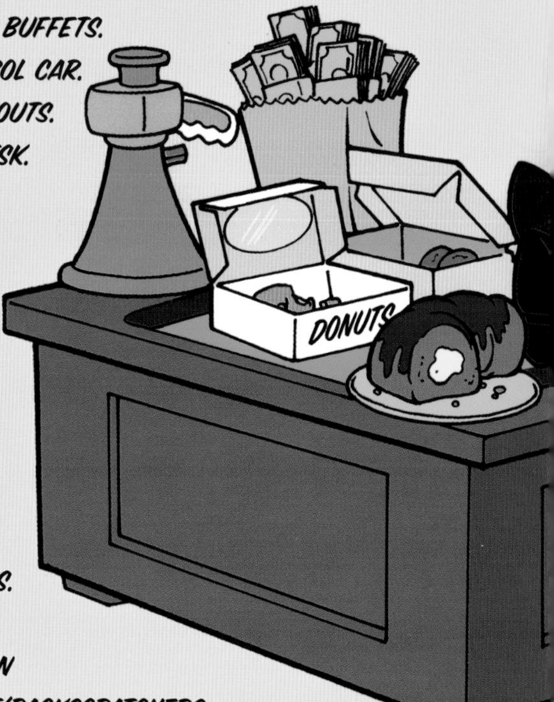
DONUTS

• In England, a boy under the age of 10 may not see a naked mannequin.

19. JAIL BREAKS.
20. COFFEE BREAKS.
21. CAKE BREAKS.
22. THE MERCILESS PEPPERS OF
QUETZALZACATENANGO.
23. THE FORBIDDEN CLOSET OF MYSTERY.
24. SELF-INCRIMINATION.
25. LOGROLLING.
26 FAT BRIBES.
27. SKINNY DIPPERS.
28. SPEED TRAPS.
29. LAGNIAPPE.
30. ADMISSIBLE EVIDENCE.
31. NO-KNOCK WARRANTS.
32. CIRCUMSTANTIAL EVIDENCE.
33. CASUAL RIOT-GEAR FRIDAYS.
34. BULLETPROOF VESTS.
35. BULLETPROOF UNDERWEAR.
36. QUID PRO QUO.
37. WATERSKIING.
38. SNOWBOARDING.
39. WATERBOARDING.
40. STUN GUNS.
41. PEDDLING MY INFLUENCE.
42. DINNER THEATER.
43. RHINO TRANQUILIZER DARTS.

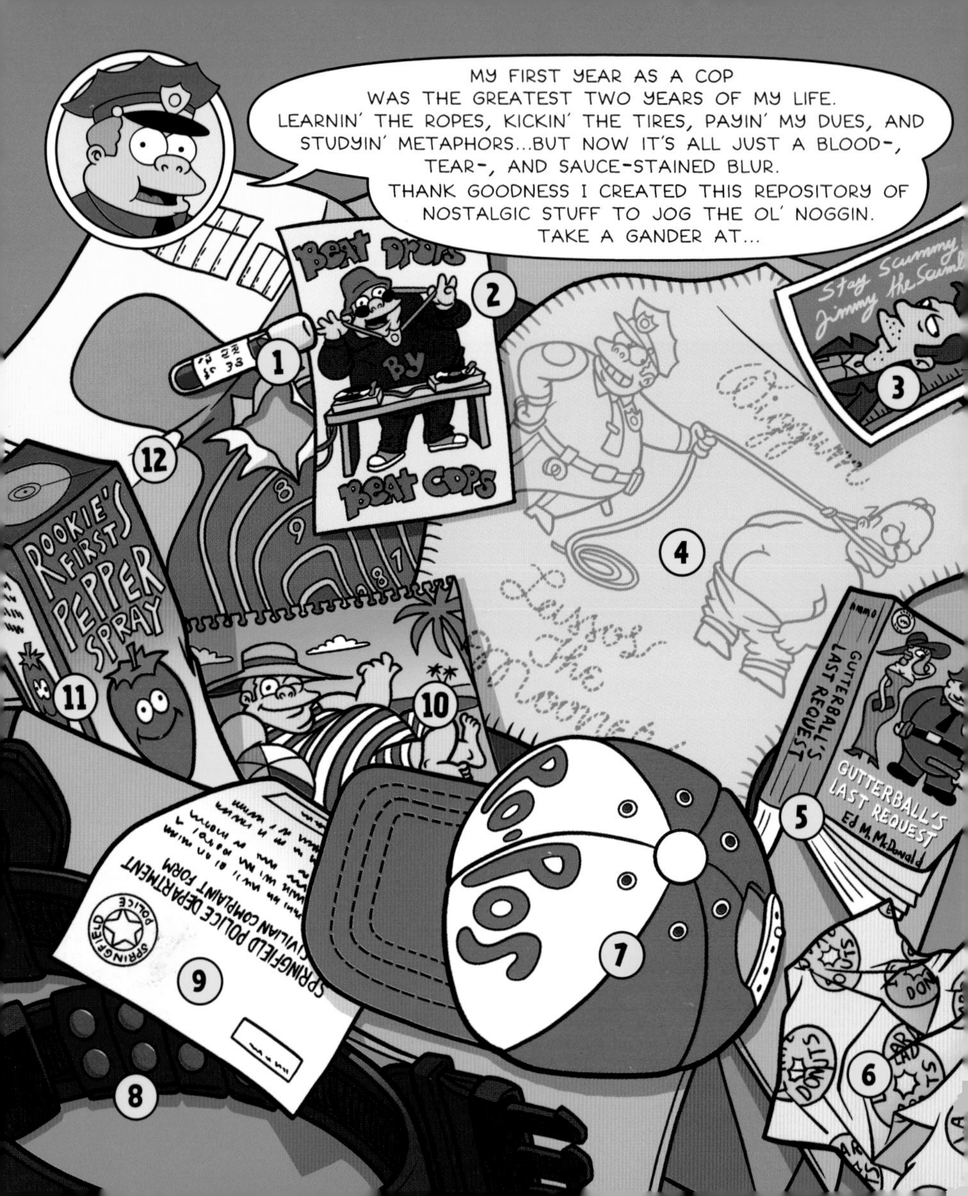
MY FIRST YEAR AS A COP
WAS THE GREATEST TWO YEARS OF MY LIFE.
LEARNIN' THE ROPES, KICKIN' THE TIRES, PAYIN' MY DUES, AND STUDYIN' METAPHORS...BUT NOW IT'S ALL JUST A BLOOD-, TEAR-, AND SAUCE-STAINED BLUR.
THANK GOODNESS I CREATED THIS REPOSITORY OF NOSTALGIC STUFF TO JOG THE OL' NOGGIN.
TAKE A GANDER AT...
BEAT DROPS
BY
BEAT COPS
Stay Scummy
Jimmy the Scumbag
ROOKIE'S FIRST PEPPER SPRAY
GUTTERBALL'S LAST REQUEST
Ed M. McDonald
SPRINGFIELD POLICE DEPARTMENT
CIVILIAN COMPLAINT FORM
SPRINGFIELD POLICE
PO-POS
DONUTS
1
2
3
4
5
6
7
8
9
10
11
12

CHIEF WIGGUM'S YEAR ONE SCRAPBOX!

1. The chief put me in charge of collecting the DNA evidence against the Camptown Ladies Killer. It was the biggest assignment of my life and a chance to redeem myself after dropping the mayor's baby. I gotta tell you, I was so proud to have the chief's vote of confidence that I just couldn't part with this blood sample!

2. Back in the day, all first-year Springfield cops were paid weekly in coupons for two free bags of flour and a box of zucchini. To get a little scratch on the side, Eddie, Lou, and I formed our own DJ crew. Our motto was, "Let the 5-0 rock your house until you have to call 911, and then we'll be here already to arrest ourselves!" Then we...er...changed it.

3. An autographed picture of my very first collar, Jimmy the Scumbag. Usually, he tries to resist arrest, but he told me mine was irresistible. Ah, that lice-ridden honey dripper...

4. I got this from a grateful art class for catching a serial mooner who harassed them for not letting him be one of their figure models. He was my first crazy.

5. As a rookie, this book was my bible. It had everything! Tough, smart cops! Beautiful dames who crack wise! Lots of pictures! And a glossary in the back for the big words!

6. The handling paper from my very first free Springfield Police HQ donut. 'Twas the sweetest maple iced I'd ever had...or will ever have. I ate it off the barrel of my gun, the way rookies are supposed to.

7. A cap from the Police Athletic League team I coached, the Springfield PD Po-Pos. They came in last place on the field, first place in pizza eating.

8. My first gun belt, size 52. I was just a beanpole!

9. The first complaint filed against me. I had commandeered a few kegs, a video projector, a satellite television receiver, a generator, and a kiddie pool. Then I cordoned off the property owner's front yard for a six-hour pay-per-view showing of the latest Drederick Tatum fight, after which I woke up in my own sick on their front stoop. Eh...people fear authority.

10. This is my shot from the "SPD Hot Cops Swimsuit Charity Calendar." We raised over twenty-seven dollars to get Gummi Bears for the break room.

11. Rookie's First Pepper Spray. Aw, my captain bought me a crate of this stuff. It features a cap that only a senior officer could open, a non-slip grip for greasy fingers, and a foolproof plunger to make sure you don't spray yourself in the face. 'Course, I still managed to a coupla times. Guess that makes me a fool. Wait. No. It doesn't...because it was proofed against fools! Game, set, and match, Wiggum!

12. The range target that certified me for police gunplay. I was so nervous that I couldn't actually hit the target with bullets, but they let me throw my service revolver at it.

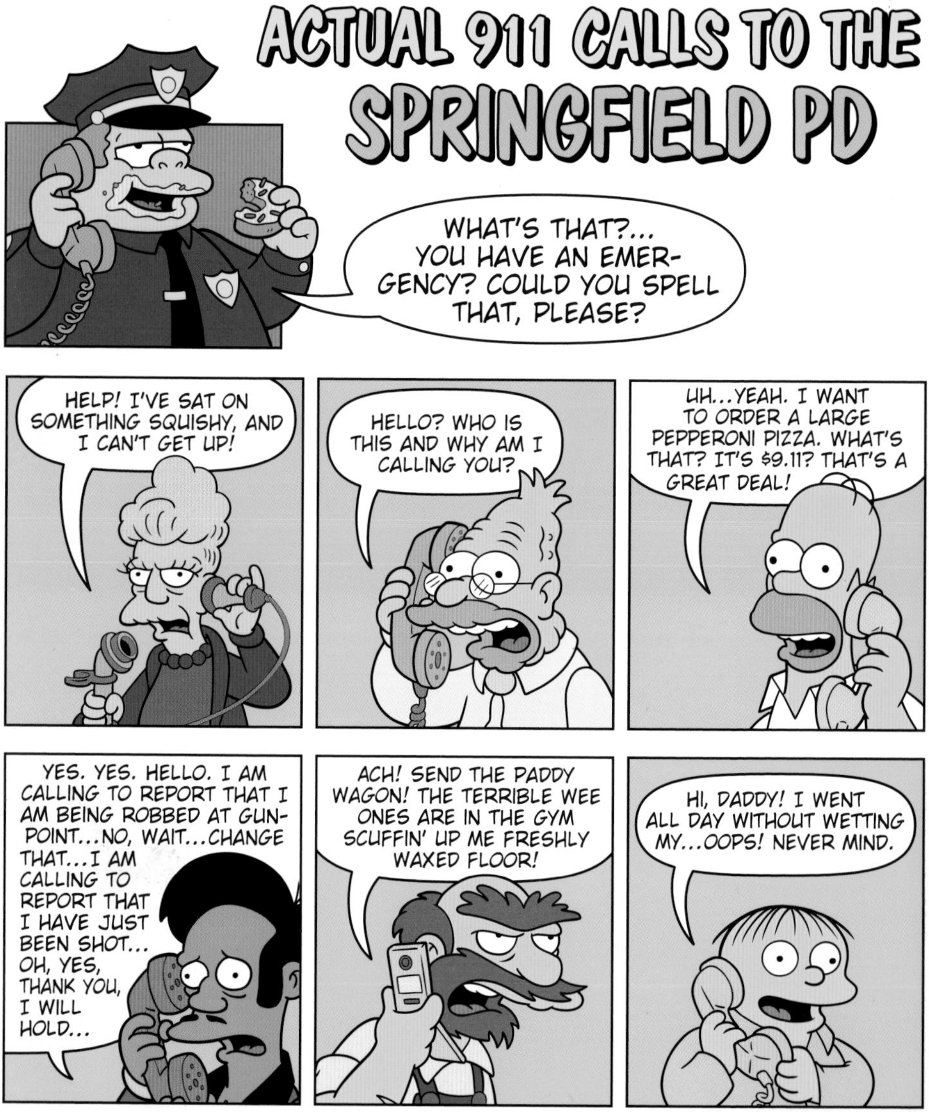
ACTUAL 911 CALLS TO THE SPRINGFIELD PD
WHAT'S THAT?... YOU HAVE AN EMERGENCY? COULD YOU SPELL THAT, PLEASE?
HELP! I'VE SAT ON SOMETHING SQUISHY, AND I CAN'T GET UP!
HELLO? WHO IS THIS AND WHY AM I CALLING YOU?
UH...YEAH. I WANT TO ORDER A LARGE PEPPERONI PIZZA. WHAT'S THAT? IT'S $9.11? THAT'S A GREAT DEAL!
YES. YES. HELLO. I AM CALLING TO REPORT THAT I AM BEING ROBBED AT GUNPOINT...NO, WAIT...CHANGE THAT...I AM CALLING TO REPORT THAT I HAVE JUST BEEN SHOT... OH, YES, THANK YOU, I WILL HOLD...
ACH! SEND THE PADDY WAGON! THE TERRIBLE WEE ONES ARE IN THE GYM SCUFFIN' UP ME FRESHLY WAXED FLOOR!
HI, DADDY! I WENT ALL DAY WITHOUT WETTING MY...OOPS! NEVER MIND.

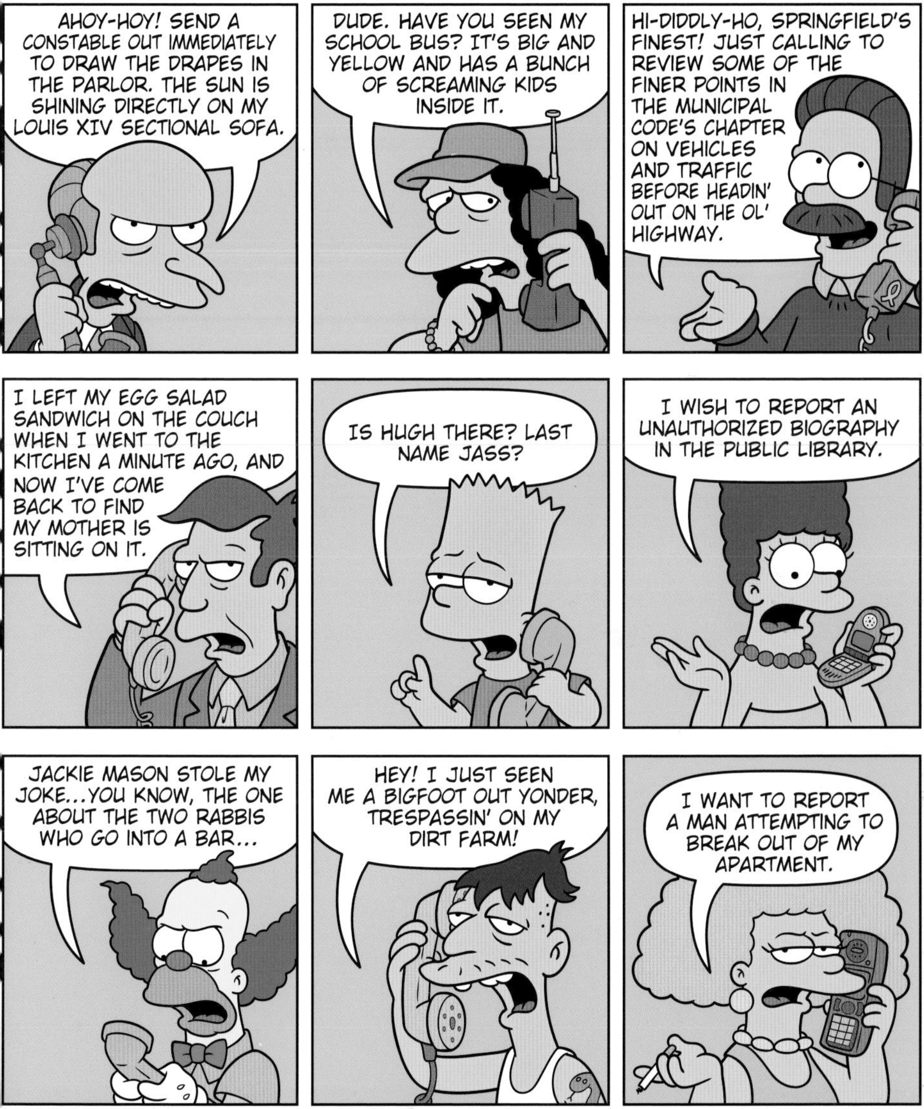
AHOY-HOY! SEND A CONSTABLE OUT IMMEDIATELY TO DRAW THE DRAPES IN THE PARLOR. THE SUN IS SHINING DIRECTLY ON MY LOUIS XIV SECTIONAL SOFA.
DUDE. HAVE YOU SEEN MY SCHOOL BUS? IT'S BIG AND YELLOW AND HAS A BUNCH OF SCREAMING KIDS INSIDE IT.
HI-DIDDLY-HO, SPRINGFIELD'S FINEST! JUST CALLING TO REVIEW SOME OF THE FINER POINTS IN THE MUNICIPAL CODE'S CHAPTER ON VEHICLES AND TRAFFIC BEFORE HEADIN' OUT ON THE OL' HIGHWAY.
I LEFT MY EGG SALAD SANDWICH ON THE COUCH WHEN I WENT TO THE KITCHEN A MINUTE AGO, AND NOW I'VE COME BACK TO FIND MY MOTHER IS SITTING ON IT.
IS HUGH THERE? LAST NAME JASS?
I WISH TO REPORT AN UNAUTHORIZED BIOGRAPHY IN THE PUBLIC LIBRARY.
JACKIE MASON STOLE MY JOKE...YOU KNOW, THE ONE ABOUT THE TWO RABBIS WHO GO INTO A BAR...
HEY! I JUST SEEN ME A BIGFOOT OUT YONDER, TRESPASSIN' ON MY DIRT FARM!
I WANT TO REPORT A MAN ATTEMPTING TO BREAK OUT OF MY APARTMENT.

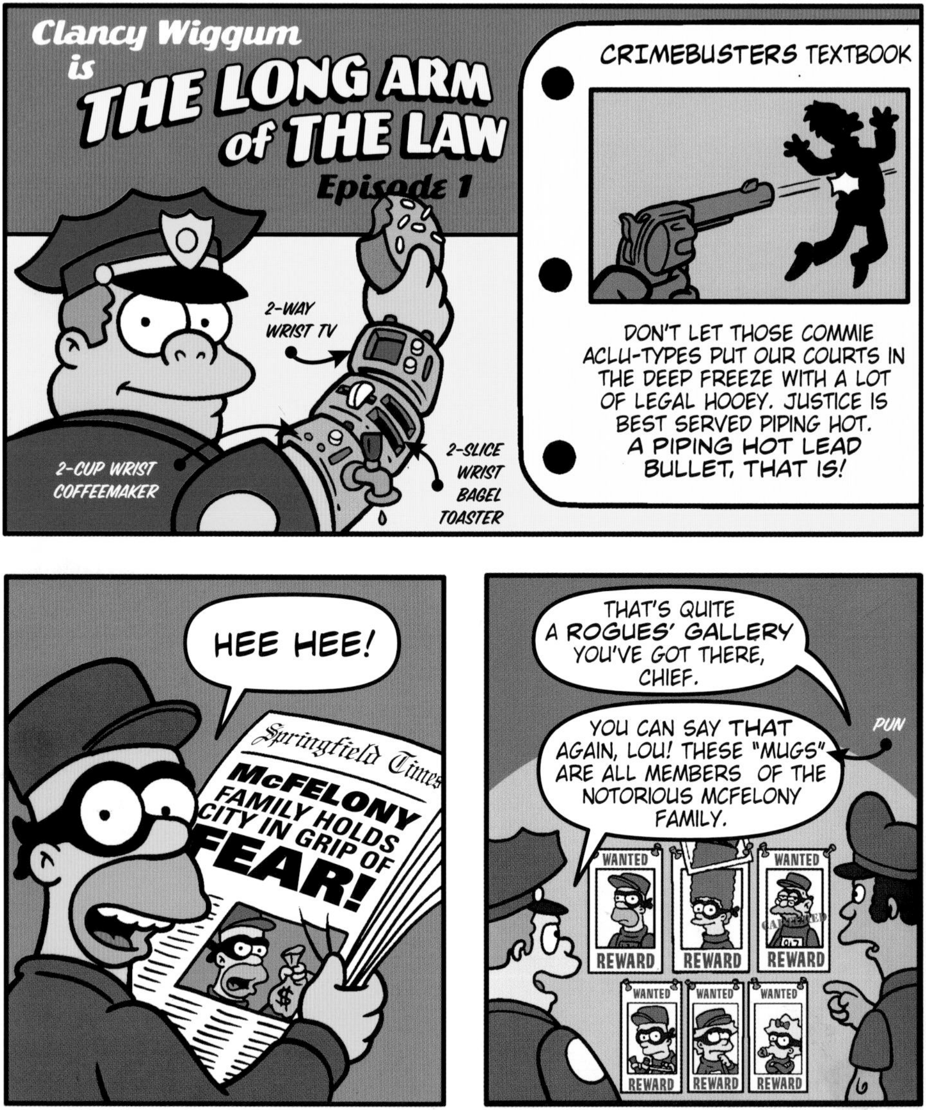

Clancy Wiggum is
THE LONG ARM of THE LAW
Episode 1
2-WAY WRIST TV
2-CUP WRIST COFFEEMAKER
2-SLICE WRIST BAGEL TOASTER
CRIMEBUSTERS TEXTBOOK
DON'T LET THOSE COMMIE ACLU-TYPES PUT OUR COURTS IN THE DEEP FREEZE WITH A LOT OF LEGAL HOOEY. JUSTICE IS BEST SERVED PIPING HOT. A PIPING HOT LEAD BULLET, THAT IS!
HEE HEE!
Springfield Times
McFELONY FAMILY HOLDS CITY IN GRIP OF FEAR!
THAT'S QUITE A ROGUES' GALLERY YOU'VE GOT THERE, CHIEF.
YOU CAN SAY THAT AGAIN, LOU! THESE "MUGS" ARE ALL MEMBERS OF THE NOTORIOUS MCFELONY FAMILY.
PUN
WANTED
REWARD
WANTED
REWARD
WANTED
REWARD
WANTED
REWARD
WANTED
REWARD
WANTED
REWARD

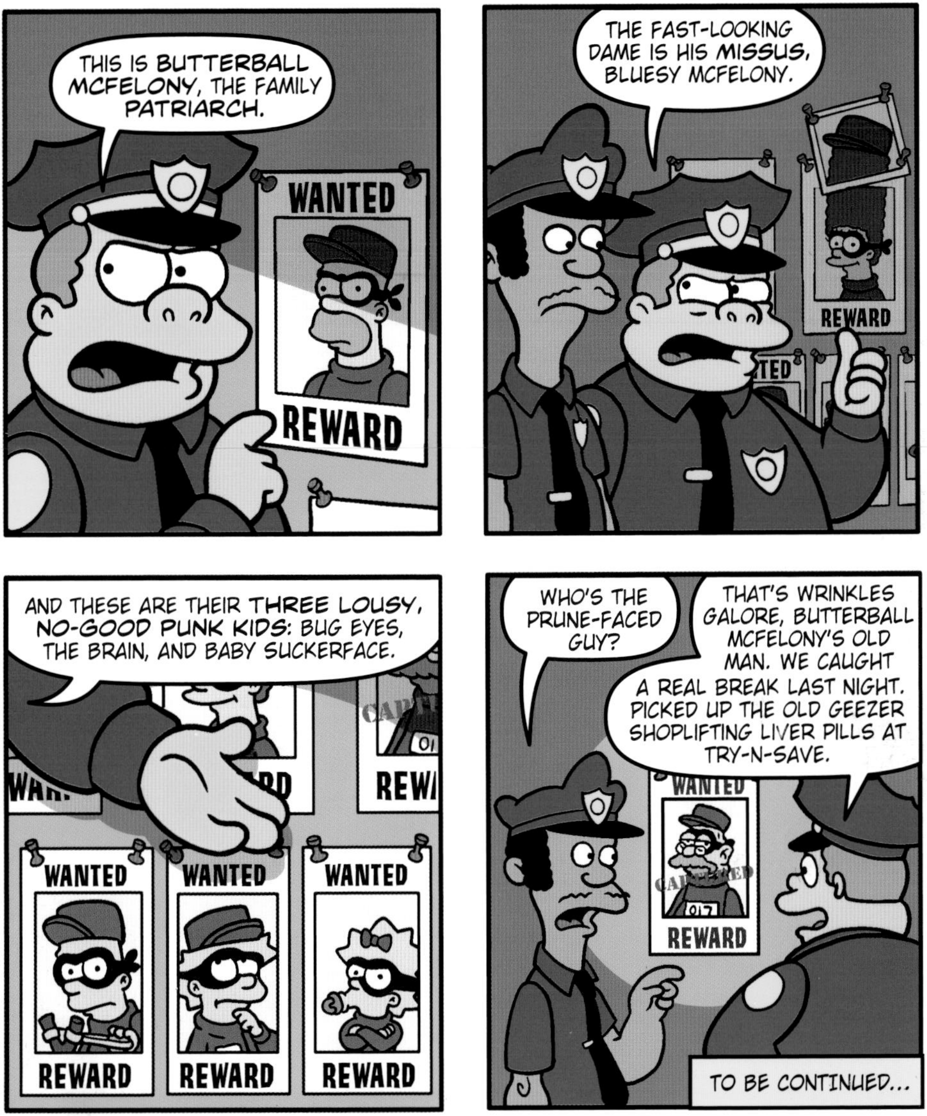
THIS IS BUTTERBALL MCFELONY, THE FAMILY PATRIARCH.
WANTED
REWARD
THE FAST-LOOKING DAME IS HIS MISSUS, BLUESY MCFELONY.
REWARD
AND THESE ARE THEIR THREE LOUSY, NO-GOOD PUNK KIDS: BUG EYES, THE BRAIN, AND BABY SUCKERFACE.
WANTED
REWARD
WANTED
REWARD
WANTED
REWARD
WHO'S THE PRUNE-FACED GUY?
THAT'S WRINKLES GALORE, BUTTERBALL MCFELONY'S OLD MAN. WE CAUGHT A REAL BREAK LAST NIGHT. PICKED UP THE OLD GEEZER SHOPLIFTING LIVER PILLS AT TRY-N-SAVE.
017
REWARD
TO BE CONTINUED...

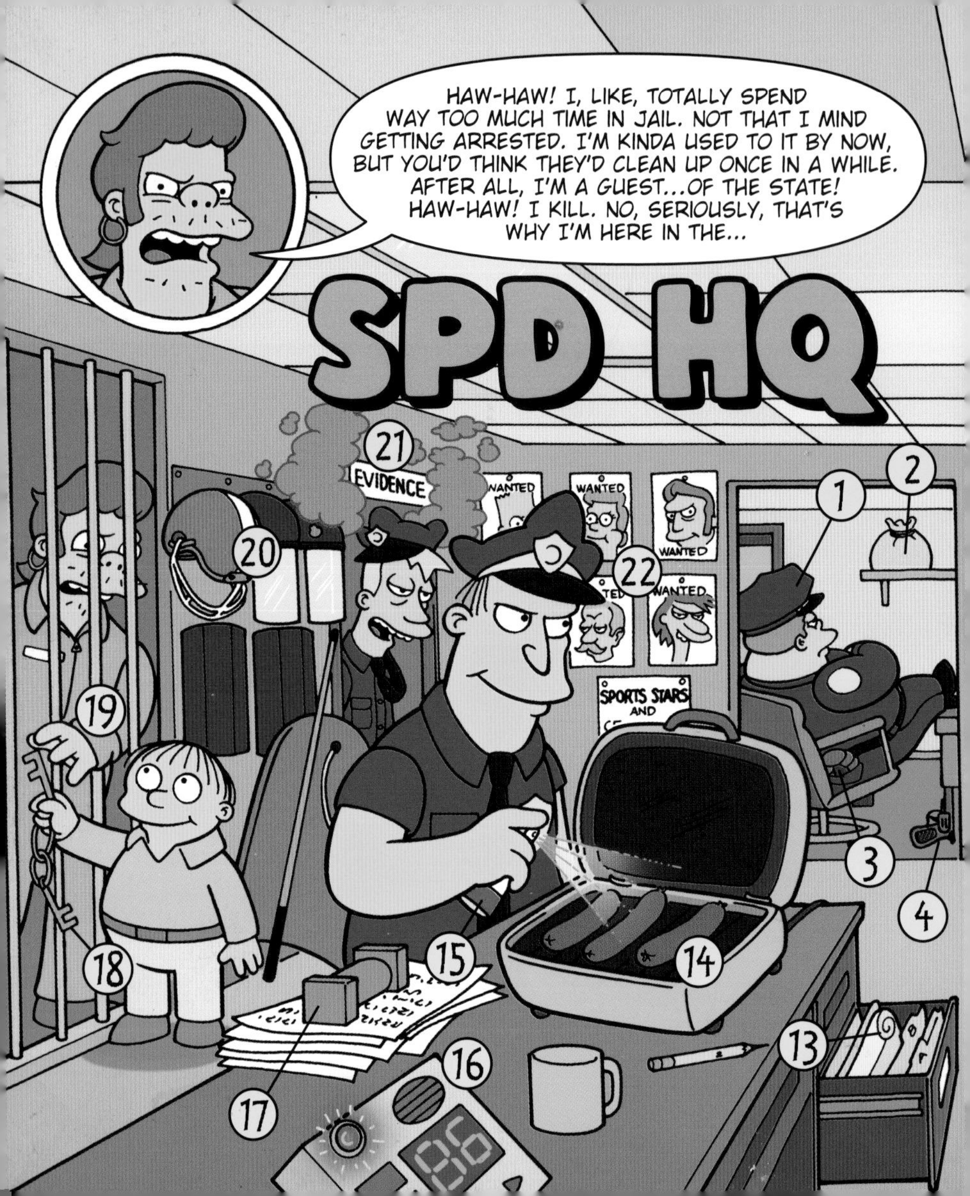
HAW-HAW! I, LIKE, TOTALLY SPEND WAY TOO MUCH TIME IN JAIL. NOT THAT I MIND GETTING ARRESTED. I'M KINDA USED TO IT BY NOW, BUT YOU'D THINK THEY'D CLEAN UP ONCE IN A WHILE. AFTER ALL, I'M A GUEST...OF THE STATE! HAW-HAW! I KILL. NO, SERIOUSLY, THAT'S WHY I'M HERE IN THE...
SPD HQ
EVIDENCE
WANTED
WANTED
WANTED
WANTED
SPORTS STARS AND
1
2
3
4
13
14
15
16
17
18
19
20
21
22

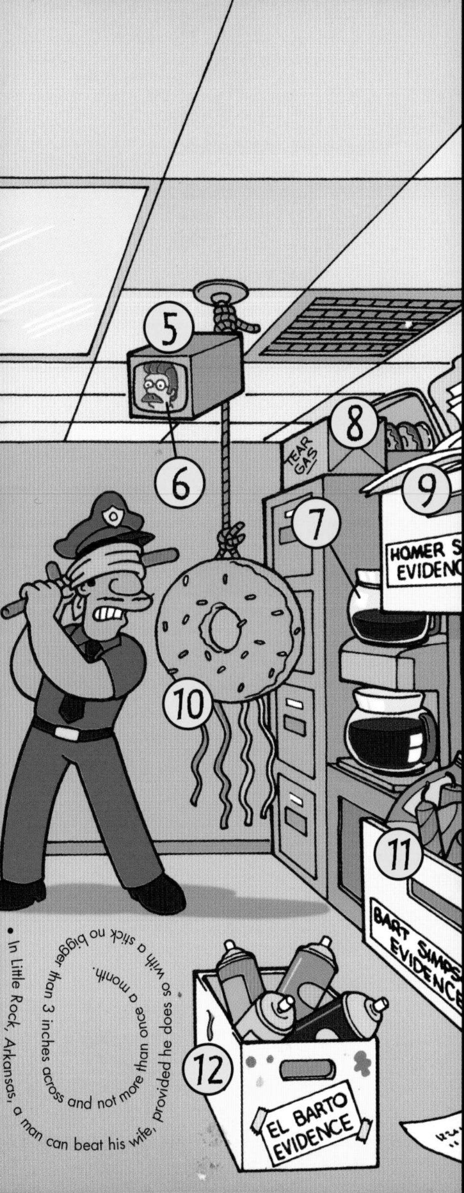
5
6
8
TEAR GAS
7
9
HOMER S
EVIDENC
10
11
BART SIMPS
EVIDENCE
12
EL BARTO EVIDENCE

• In Little Rock, Arkansas, a man can beat his wife, provided he does so with a stick no bigger than 3 inches across and not more than once a month.

1. Chief Wiggum
2. Bribe sack
3. Year-old cruller
4. Police revolver
5. Interrogation Room monitor
6. Stoolie
7. Two-month-old pot of coffee
8. Secret donut stash
9. Homer Simpson's filing cabinet
10. Police piñata
11. Bart Simpson's fireworks
12. El Barto evidence
13. Burrito
14. Spicy pepper spray dogs
15. Pepper spray
16. 911 answering machine
17. Stun grenade
18. Prison keys
19. Suspect
20. Riot gear
21. Evidence Room
22. Wanted posters

THE SPD AUCTION

"GOOD BUYS FROM BAD GUYS!"

SCARFACE: THE COLOGNE

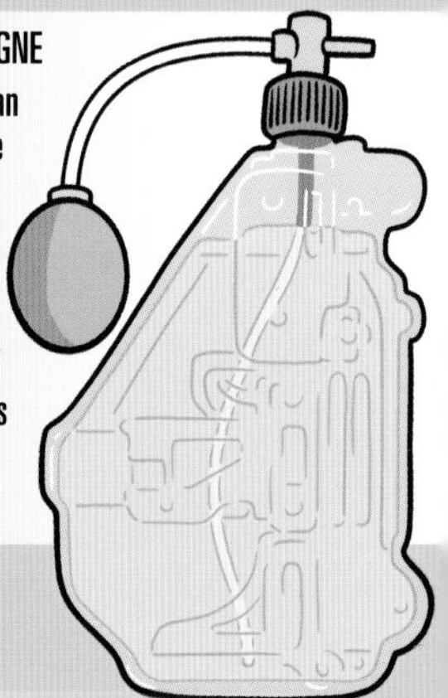

Just because you don't live the horrific, violent life of a paranoid drug lord doesn't mean you can't smell like one! Capture the essence of a criminal legend with this signature cologne. Exuding an aroma of sandalwood, gunpowder, and pine car freshener, this is a scent that will say to people, "Stay away from me! I'm an unhinged, remorseless sociopath who knows how to dress!" This cologne's powerful odor will be saying "Hello" to your little and large friends several blocks before you actually arrive.

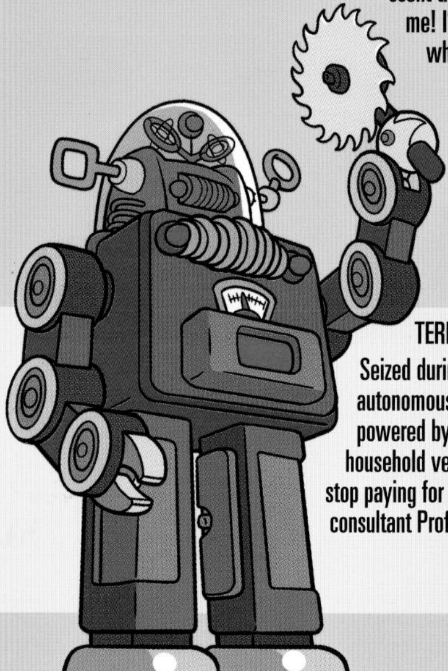

TERRORBOT

Seized during a raid on Dr. Colossus' mountain stronghold, this twelve-foot-high, fully autonomous, artificially intelligent robot is equipped with an array of weapons and is powered by a miniature fusion chamber. TerrorBot can be programmed to execute household vermin AND household chores! Kick out your cleaning lady, ditch your dog, and stop paying for home security. TerrorBot can ensure a tidy, safe abode, and, according to SPD consultant Professor Frink, there is a 50 percent possibility that TerrorBot can love!!!

(WARNING: Winning bidders will immediately be responsible for any civic destruction caused due to TerrorBot negligence, glitches, programming errors, or emerging sentience.)

2,000 LBS. OF FROZEN FREE-RANGE ALPACA MEAT

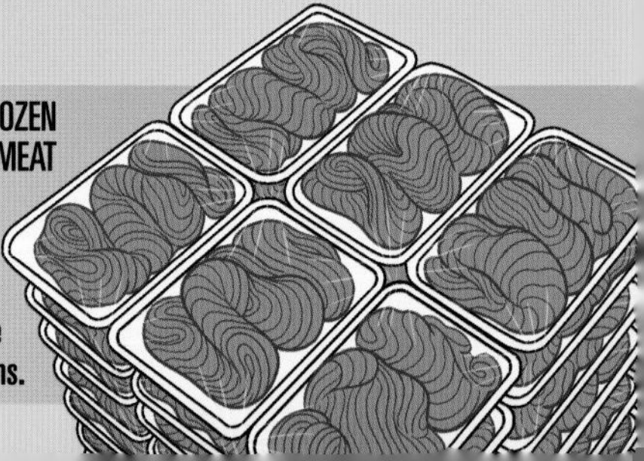

Confiscated as a result of a "100% All-Beef Hamburger" fraud operation by a local clown-owned fast-food chain, this free-range alpaca meat is actually healthier than most commercial beef. Low in fat, hormone-free, and delightfully stringy, the deerlike flesh will keep your family fed for months.

REE HAMMERHEAD SHARKS AND A TWO-MONTH SUPPLY OF DICK VAN PATTEN'S ALL-NATURAL ORGANIC CHUM

An opportunity of a lifetime! How many times have you aid to yourself, "Damn, I want me three sharks and plenty of their favorite organic chum, too!" Well, your sinking ship full of plump survivors has come in! These little chompers were eized from a black-market shark-fin soup outfit operating in the basement of Moe's Tavern. These hammies are PRICED TO MOVE!

(NOTE: Tank not included; bids will have to include proof of large aquarium or swimming pool ownership.)

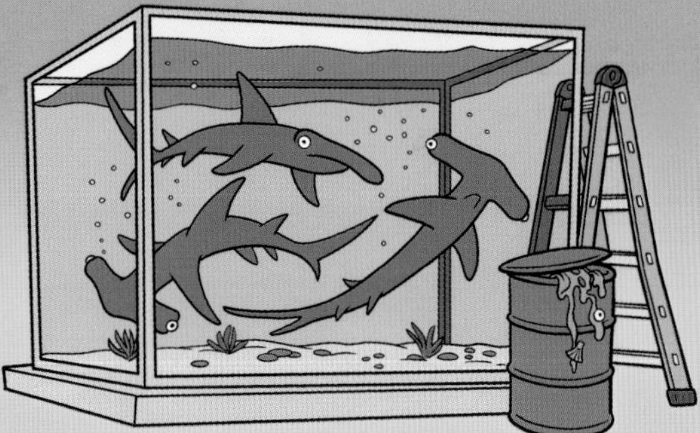

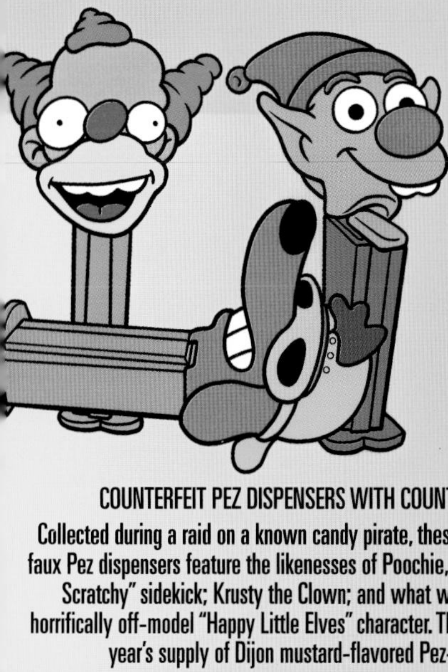

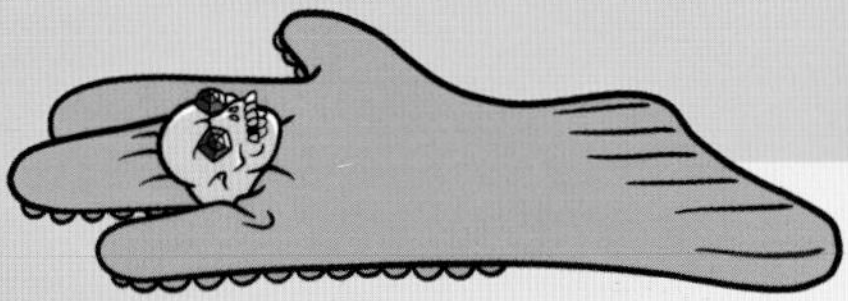

EVIL CAT STROKING/DESHEDDING GLOVE

Do you enjoy stroking a longhair cat while evilly discussing or contemplating dastardly plans? Use that time to groom your cat as well! Recovered from an asthmatic supervillain, this Evil Cat Stroking/Deshedding Glove collects loose cat hair and dander to help your #1 henchcat become hypoallergenic! Built into the glove is a platinum ruby ring to project malevolent authority and style!

COUNTERFEIT PEZ DISPENSERS WITH COUNTERFEIT PEZ

Collected during a raid on a known candy pirate, these 15,000-of-a-kind faux Pez dispensers feature the likenesses of Poochie, the hilarious "Itchy & Scratchy" sidekick; Krusty the Clown; and what we believe to be a horrifically off-model "Happy Little Elves" character. They also come with a year's supply of Dijon mustard-flavored Pez-like candy.

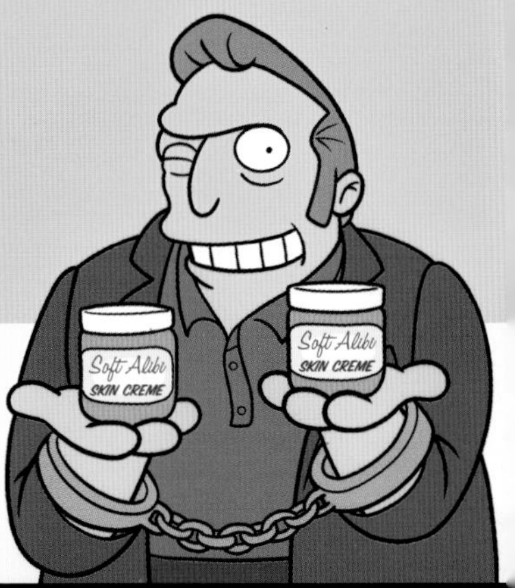
Soft Alibi
SKIN CREME
Soft Alibi
SKIN CREME

FAT TONY'S SOFT ALIBI SKIN CREME

The SPD has acquired over two thousand tubs of this rich, silky moisturizer, specifically formulated to fight the chafing, flaking, and redness brought on by handcuffs. Now, you can share in the secret that has kept "legitimate businessman" Fat Tony's wrists soft and flexible through twenty years of criminal prosecution!

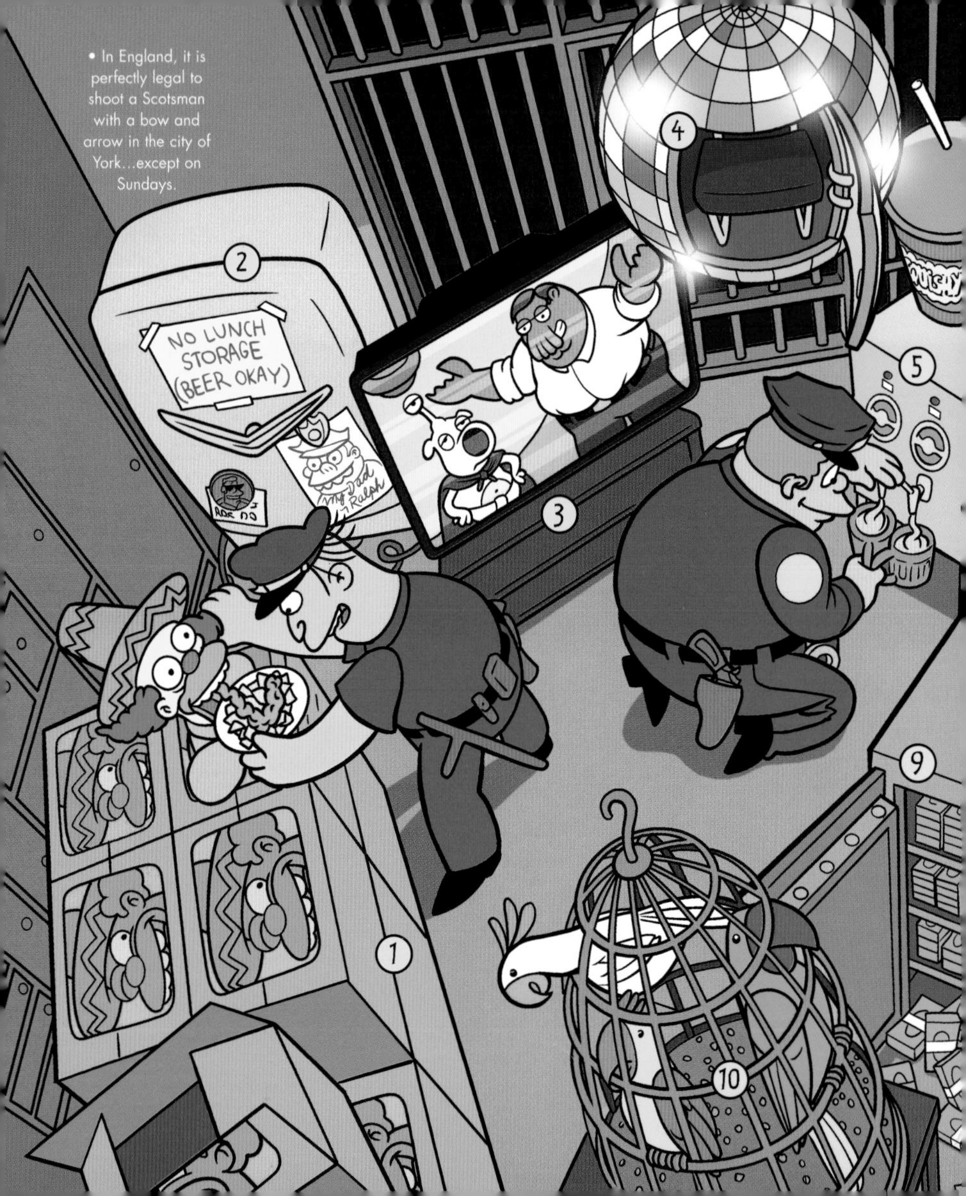
• In England, it is perfectly legal to shoot a Scotsman with a bow and arrow in the city of York…except on Sundays.
NO LUNCH STORAGE (BEER OKAY)
My Dad by Ralph
SQUISHY
1
2
3
4
5
9
10

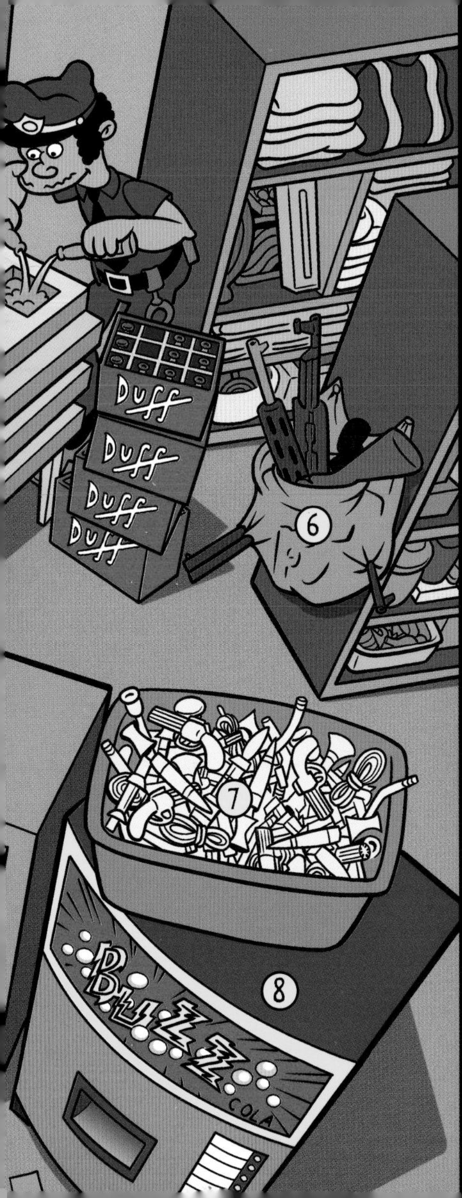

Duff
Duff
Duff
Duff
6
7
8
Buzz
COLA

It is one of the most secure places in Springfield, a room in which material proof of criminal activity is cataloged, stored, and occasionally played with a little bit! Behold, the contents of...

THE SPRINGFIELD POLICE DEPARTMENT'S EVIDENCE LOCKER!

1. Knockoff Krusty Head Honcho Nacho Cheese dispenser heads. (It was determined they were counterfeit when they were found to work perfectly and pose no danger of electrical shock or viral meningitis.)
2. Evidence fridge (for perishable samples and evidence: inside are vials of all manner of bodily fluids and solids, crime-oriented foodstuffs, body parts, and ice-cold drinks).
3. Flatscreen TV (used for reviewing pirated, cheap knockoff DVDs and games) here showing an episode of "Future Guy."
4. A two-way mirrorball (confiscated from one of Fat Tony's illegal gaming halls. Apparently, the mob used it for cheating by concealing a little person in the ball above a poker table with binoculars and a walkie-talkie.).
5. Squishee machine (seized from the Kwik-E-Mart for assault on an officer after it gave Lou brain freeze).
6. The gunny sack (contains confiscated munitions, from shotguns to slingshots).
7. Clue bin.
8. Counterfeit bill tester.
9. Counterfeit money storage.
10. Various parrot witnesses.

The Fat Blue Line

"Taking Out Crime, One Bite at a Time."

A POLICEMAN'S GUIDE TO WHERE TO EAT FOR FREE IN SPRINGFIELD

IZZY'S DELI
So what's not to like?

P. PIGGLY HOGSWINE'S SUPER-SMØRG
The food's good, but their all-you-can-eat policy takes the fun out of freeloading.

GULP 'N' BLOW
Great for a quick meal when you're on your way to an emergency call.

JITTERY JOE'S COFFEE SHOP
If it weren't free, we wouldn't eat here if you paid us.

LUIGI'S
We've said it again and again—Chef Luigi's signature Pizza di Polizia is sure to repeat on you!

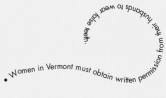

• Women in Vermont must obtain written permission from their husbands to wear false teeth.

KRUSTYBURGER
Stay away from the Krusty Nuggets until the boys at the crime lab determine the ingredients.

🍩🌙

GREASY JOE'S BOTTOMLESS BAR-B-Q PIT
We can't say much for the food, but their patented BBQ grease technology provides top-quality barrel lubrication for all department-issue firearms.

🍩

LARD LAD
Advise all units: Lard Lad never pays off on their "Betcha can't eat eight dozen!" slogan.

🍩🍩

MUNICIPAL HOUSE OF PANCAKES
Be sure to try the flapjacks with Halleberry syrup…or, if you're feeling a little phlegmish, ask for the prescription Koff syrup.

🍩🍩🍩

FACESTUFFERS
Go easy on the tomato sauce—the homicide detectives say it's murder on the upholstery.

🍩🍩🌙

THE TEXAS CHEESECAKE DEPOSITORY
For you single-officer patrols, we recommend the Lone Gunman Special (with extra garlic).

🍩🍩🍩🍩🍩

JAVA THE HUT
You just can't beat the taste of a free cup of overpriced coffee!

🍩🍩🍩🌙

RATINGS GUIDE		
🍩🍩🍩🍩🍩	-----	GREAT, BUT COULD BE BETTER.
🍩🍩🍩🍩	-------	GOOD, BUT NOT GREAT.
🍩🍩🍩	----------	NOT SO GOOD, BUT NOT SO BAD, EITHER.
🍩🍩	-----------	BAD, BUT WE'VE HAD WORSE.
🍩	-------------	TERRIBLE, BUT IT'S FREE.

SPRINGFIELD'S

If you have any information regarding any of the following suspects, or if you just feel like squealing on a neighbor or ratting out a coworker, please call us at **1-800-IBA-FINK**.

Cletus Del Roy Spuckler
a.k.a. Cletus the Slack-Jawed Yokel

Wanted on suspicion of numerous hillbilly clichés, including operating an illegal moonshine still out by the cement pond.
DESCRIPTION: Slack-jawed yokel.
CAUTION: Has been known to lead "revenooers" on a wild chase set to old-timey banjo music.

Maggie Simpson

Wanted on suspicion of the attempted murder of Charles Montgomery Burns.
DESCRIPTION: Adorable.
CAUTION: Suspect is considered armed and extremely cranky if she doesn't get her nap.

Otto Mann
a.k.a. Otto, man; the Bus Driver

Wanted on suspicion of possession of marijuana, grass, pot, weed, chronic, Mary Jane, hemp, cannabis, ganja, joints, doobies, and reefer.
DESCRIPTION: Kind of a cross between a swinging hippie freak and a totally '80s headbanger dude.
CAUTION: Suspect stops at all railroad crossings.

MOST WANTED

Waylon J. Smithers, Jr.

Wanted on suspicion of excessive foot tapping in the men's room at Springfield Airport.

DESCRIPTION: Neat dresser. A little too neat, if you catch our drift.

CAUTION: Suspect has been known to assume an inappropriately wide stance.

Snake a.k.a. Jailbird

Wanted on suspicion of robbery, burglary, breaking and entering and leaving with a bunch of stuff that doesn't belong to him.

DESCRIPTION: A seedy version of one of those guys on "Beverly Hills, 90210."

CAUTION: Has escaped from Springfield Reformatory, Springfield Jail, Springfield High School Detention Room, and the Springfield Pound.

Robert Underdunk Terwilliger a.k.a. Sideshow Bob

Wanted on suspicion of homicidal mania and unbridled pomposity.

DESCRIPTION: Looks like a redheaded Rastaman—you can't miss him!

CAUTION: Suspect considered to be well-armed and big-footed.

Lucille Botzcowski
a.k.a. Ms. Botz, the Babysitter Bandit

Wanted on suspicion of home invasion, robbery, and babysitting without a permit.
DESCRIPTION: Vile-looking hag that only the most desperate of parents would hire to babysit their children.
CAUTION: Charges extra for kids under two years of age.

Jonathan Schmallippe
a.k.a. Johnny Tightlips

Wanted on suspicion of racketeering, including supplying rat's milk to the school cafeteria, selling illegal fireworks, and scoffing at the law.
DESCRIPTION: Extremely tight lips.
CAUTION: Suspect is a member in good standing of the Legitimate Businessman's Social Club and a close personal friend of Mayor Quimby.

Groundskeeper Willie

Wanted on suspicion of peeping tomfoolery and improper relations with a tractor.
DESCRIPTION: A stereotypical kilt-wearing, haggis-eating, splenetic Scotsman with a fierce shock of flaming red hair.
CAUTION: Suspect is a stereotypical kilt-wearing, haggis-eating, splenetic Scotsman with a fierce temper.

Cecil Terwilliger

Wanted on suspicion of being a dam liar in regards to his shoddy hydrodynamical engineering project. DESCRIPTION: Also wanted on suspicion of wearing an argyle vest. CAUTION: Member of the notorious Terwilliger crime family.

Herman

Wanted for possession of a small-scale tactical nuclear anti-beatnik bomb. DESCRIPTION: Has only one arm. CAUTION: Ironically, suspect considered to be well-armed.

• In Texas, it is against the law to milk another person's cow.

Eleanor Abernathy
a.k.a. Crazy Cat Lady

Wanted on suspicion of cat flinging with intent to cause bodily harm to passersby. DESCRIPTION: Crazy-looking lady with cats. CAUTION: Suspect is believed to be in possession of a degree from Yale Law School.

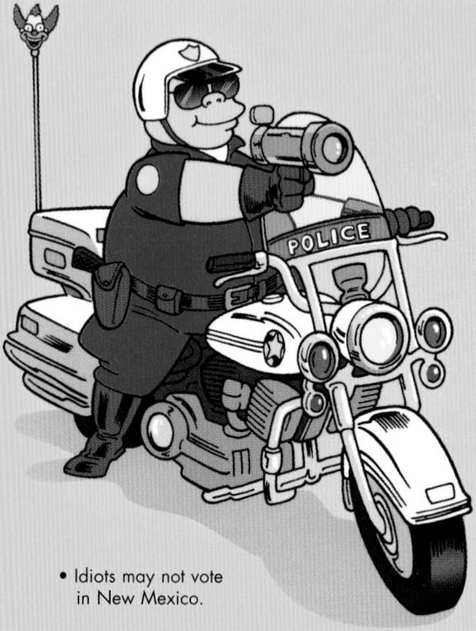
POLICE

• Idiots may not vote in New Mexico.

CLANCY WIGGUM'S TEN RULES FOR AVOIDING A SPEEDING TICKET

RULE 1. Don't speed. Cops give out very few speeding tickets to people who drive at or below the speed limit—unless you drive really slow and you're in our way. Then we'll pull your ass over, too.

RULE 2. Don't speed where you're likely to get caught. In other words, don't speed around cops. Limit your speeding to high-crime neighborhoods that cops avoid and times when there are no Springfield cops working (usually Wednesday nights and weekends).

RULE 3. Don't let cops see you speeding. If you're driving at high speed at night, you'd be smart to turn off your headlights. During the day, it's a little harder to hide, but if you have a cloaking device, use it.

RULE 4. Use common sense. Cops can't tell how fast you're going any more than you can, but we have one thing you probably don't—a radar gun. But it doesn't work during gamma radiation storms or when it's on loan to the Isotopes for a home game. (Hint, hint.)

RULE 5. Don't get caught. Okay, so we've clocked you going 90 on the gun, and we're in a high-speed pursuit. You know your car can go 90 and our fastest cruiser is a '98 Olds that pegs the speedometer at 85. You do the math.

RULE 6. Be a cop. Ever notice how fast cops drive? Doesn't matter whether we're rushing to answer an urgent cry for help or just looking for a cheap thrill, we're the envy of bats out of Hell everywhere. But have you ever seen a cop pull another cop over for speeding? I haven't. And I'm a cop.

RULE 7. Have a good excuse. If you do get pulled over, at least put some thought into what you say to the officer. Things like: "I had to pee bad" won't get you as far as "I wanted you to pull me over, so I could reward a handsome officer like you with this crisp new $100 bill."

RULE 8. Be polite and respectful. Cops are human, too. They like to be treated with dignity and compassion. They enjoy the warm caress of an attractive blonde in a tight blouse and short skirt, with a soft spot for a man in a uniform. That mostly only works for women, though.

RULE 9. Best defense is a good offense. If a cop has you dead to rights for speeding, act drunk. Fall out of the car, stumble around sloppily, and if you can spontaneously vomit your guts out, do. No cop worth his badge will give you a speeding ticket.

RULE 10. When all else fails. If you get a ticket, you can always miss the court date, have a bench warrant issued against you, and, when the cops come to serve it, get killed in a violent shootout. Judges usually go easy on corpses. You'll probably just get traffic school.

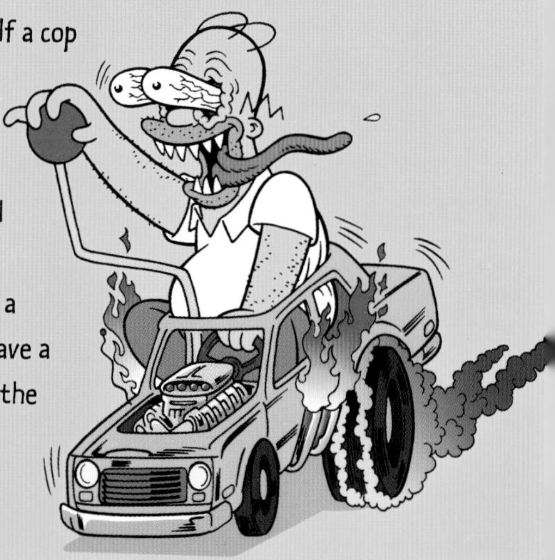

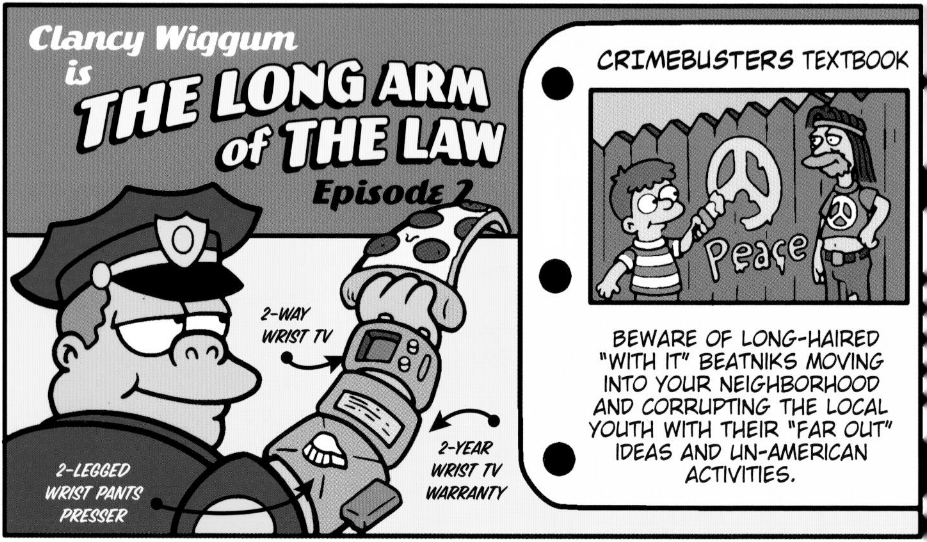
Clancy Wiggum
is
THE LONG ARM of THE LAW
Episode 2
2-WAY WRIST TV
2-YEAR WRIST TV WARRANTY
2-LEGGED WRIST PANTS PRESSER
CRIMEBUSTERS TEXTBOOK
peace
BEWARE OF LONG-HAIRED "WITH IT" BEATNIKS MOVING INTO YOUR NEIGHBORHOOD AND CORRUPTING THE LOCAL YOUTH WITH THEIR "FAR OUT" IDEAS AND UN-AMERICAN ACTIVITIES.

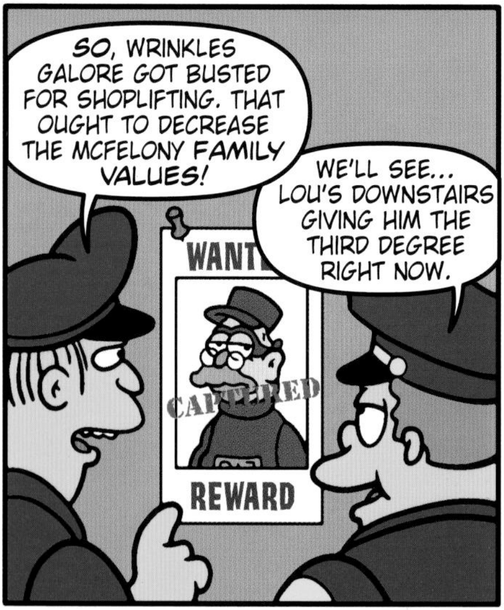
SO, WRINKLES GALORE GOT BUSTED FOR SHOPLIFTING. THAT OUGHT TO DECREASE THE MCFELONY FAMILY VALUES!
WE'LL SEE... LOU'S DOWNSTAIRS GIVING HIM THE THIRD DEGREE RIGHT NOW.
REWARD

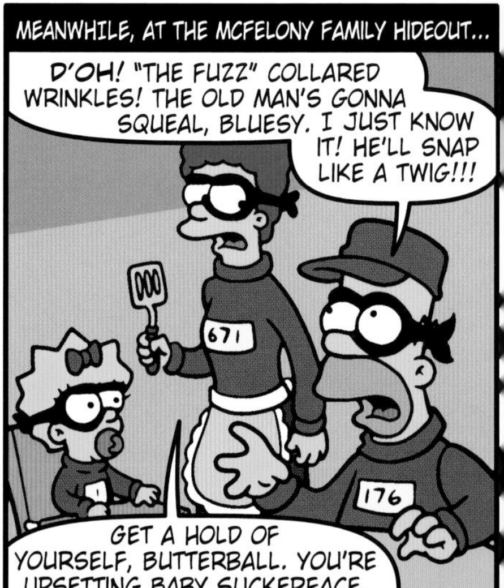
MEANWHILE, AT THE MCFELONY FAMILY HIDEOUT...
D'OH! "THE FUZZ" COLLARED WRINKLES! THE OLD MAN'S GONNA SQUEAL, BLUESY. I JUST KNOW IT! HE'LL SNAP LIKE A TWIG!!!
671
176
GET A HOLD OF YOURSELF, BUTTERBALL. YOU'RE UPSETTING BABY SUCKERFACE.

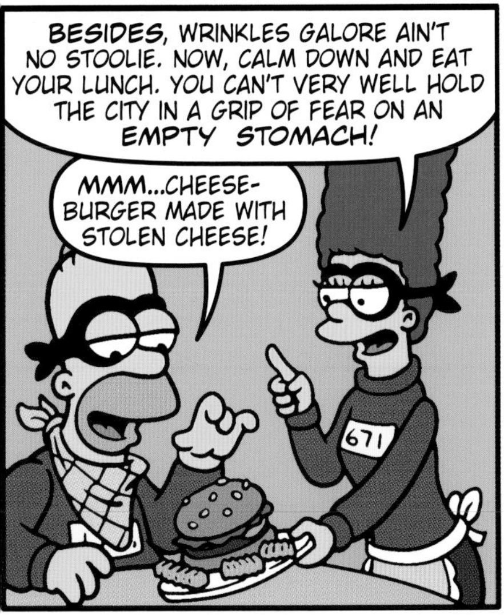
BESIDES, WRINKLES GALORE AIN'T NO STOOLIE. NOW, CALM DOWN AND EAT YOUR LUNCH. YOU CAN'T VERY WELL HOLD THE CITY IN A GRIP OF FEAR ON AN EMPTY STOMACH!
MMM...CHEESE-BURGER MADE WITH STOLEN CHEESE!
671

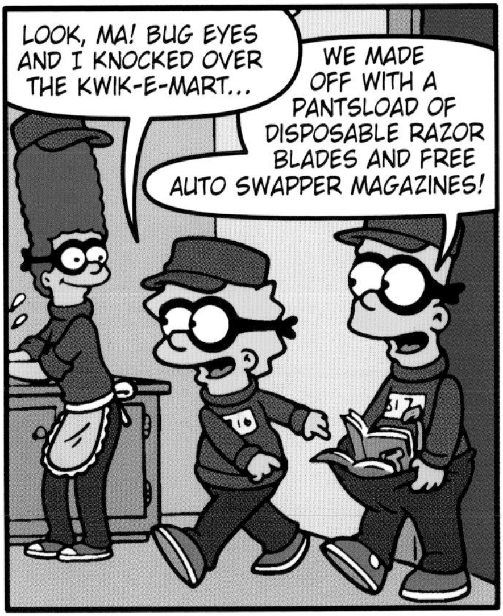
LOOK, MA! BUG EYES AND I KNOCKED OVER THE KWIK-E-MART...
WE MADE OFF WITH A PANTSLOAD OF DISPOSABLE RAZOR BLADES AND FREE AUTO SWAPPER MAGAZINES!

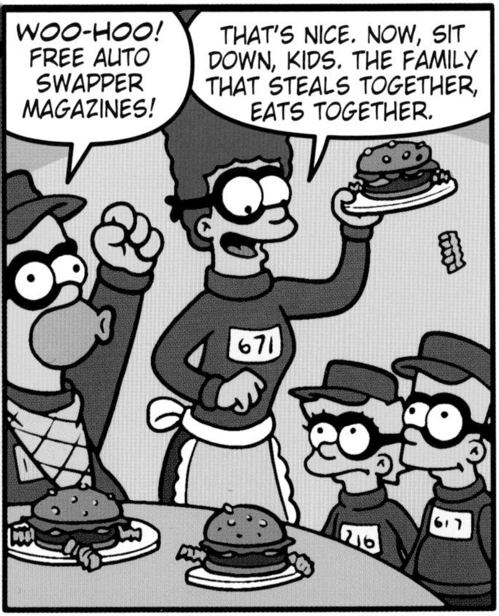
WOO-HOO! FREE AUTO SWAPPER MAGAZINES!
THAT'S NICE. NOW, SIT DOWN, KIDS. THE FAMILY THAT STEALS TOGETHER, EATS TOGETHER.
671
216
617

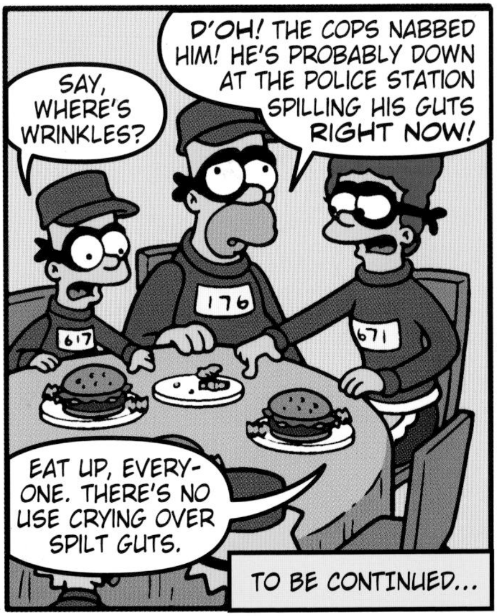
SAY, WHERE'S WRINKLES?
D'OH! THE COPS NABBED HIM! HE'S PROBABLY DOWN AT THE POLICE STATION SPILLING HIS GUTS RIGHT NOW!
617
176
671
EAT UP, EVERY-ONE. THERE'S NO USE CRYING OVER SPILT GUTS.
TO BE CONTINUED...

JAIL vs. SCHOOL

Combination stainless-steel sink/toilet/chair/desk

Bunks mounted to the walls

Cruel and unusual punishment

You have the right to remain silent

Strip searches

Fenced-in exercise yard

Three Strikes law

Solitary confinement

Lockdown

Mandatory sentencing

Electronic monitoring

Time off for good behavior

Work-release program

Parole

• Tags may be legally removed from pillows and mattresses in Colorado.

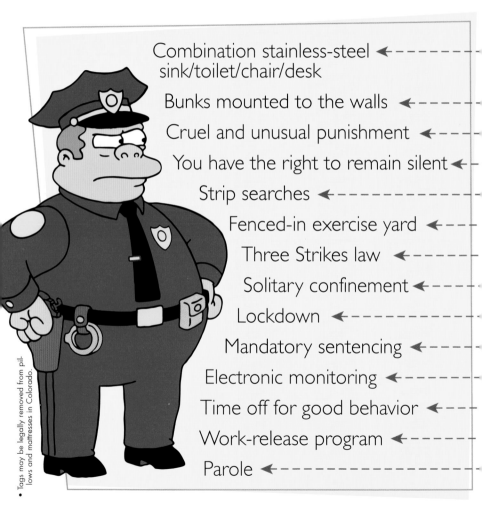

Which Is Worse?

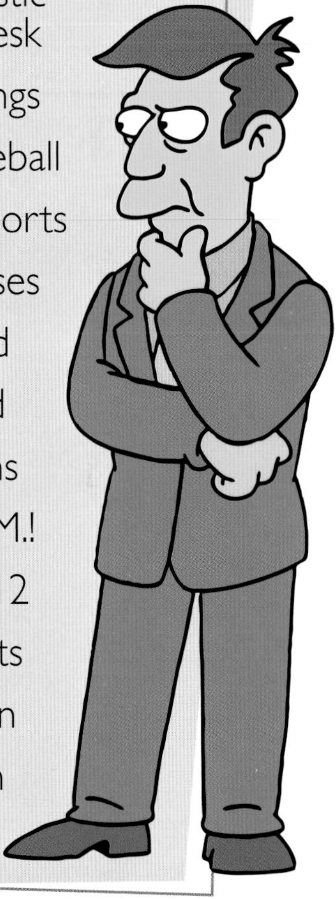

Blow-molded plastic combination chair/desk

Asbestos attached to the ceilings

Dodgeball

Oral reports

Gym classes

Fenced-in playground

No Child Left Behind

Weekends and summer vacations

Life begins at 3:00 P.M.!

K-12

Sending a note home to parents

Detention

Suspension

Expulsion

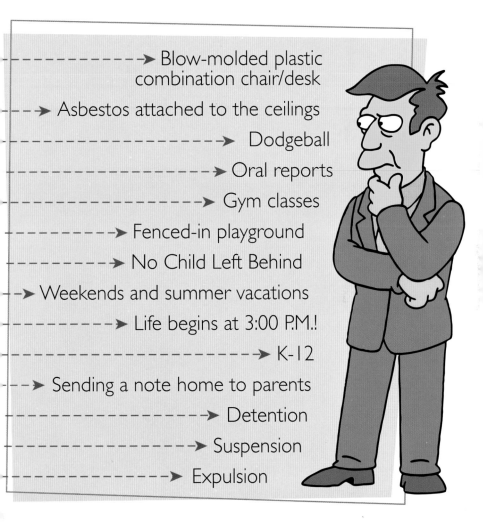

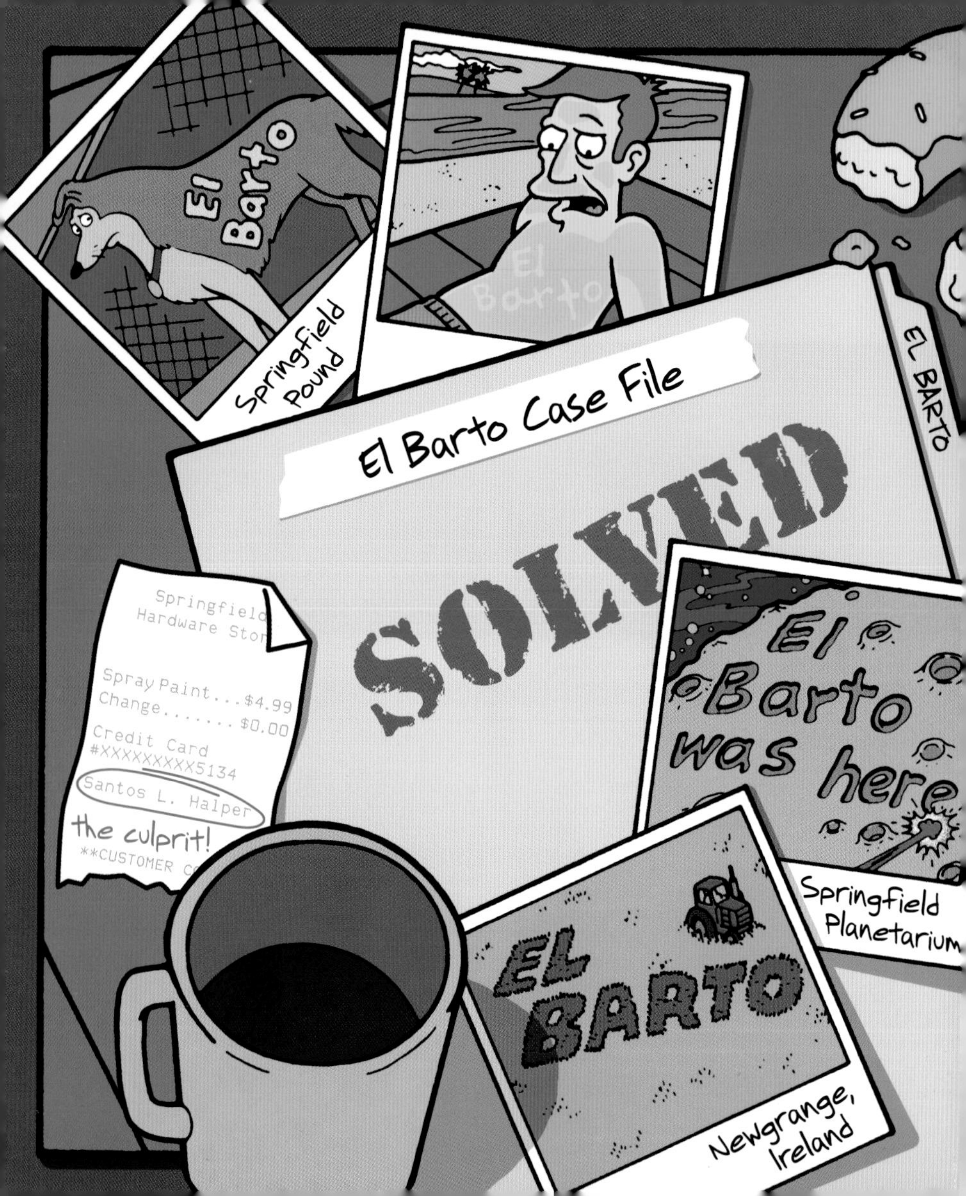

El Barto
Springfield Pound
El Barto
El Barto Case File
EL BARTO
SOLVED
Springfield Hardware Store
Spray Paint...$4.99
Change.......$0.00
Credit Card
#XXXXXXXXX5134
Santos L. Halper
the culprit!
**CUSTOMER CO
El Barto was here
Springfield Planetarium
EL BARTO
Newgrange, Ireland

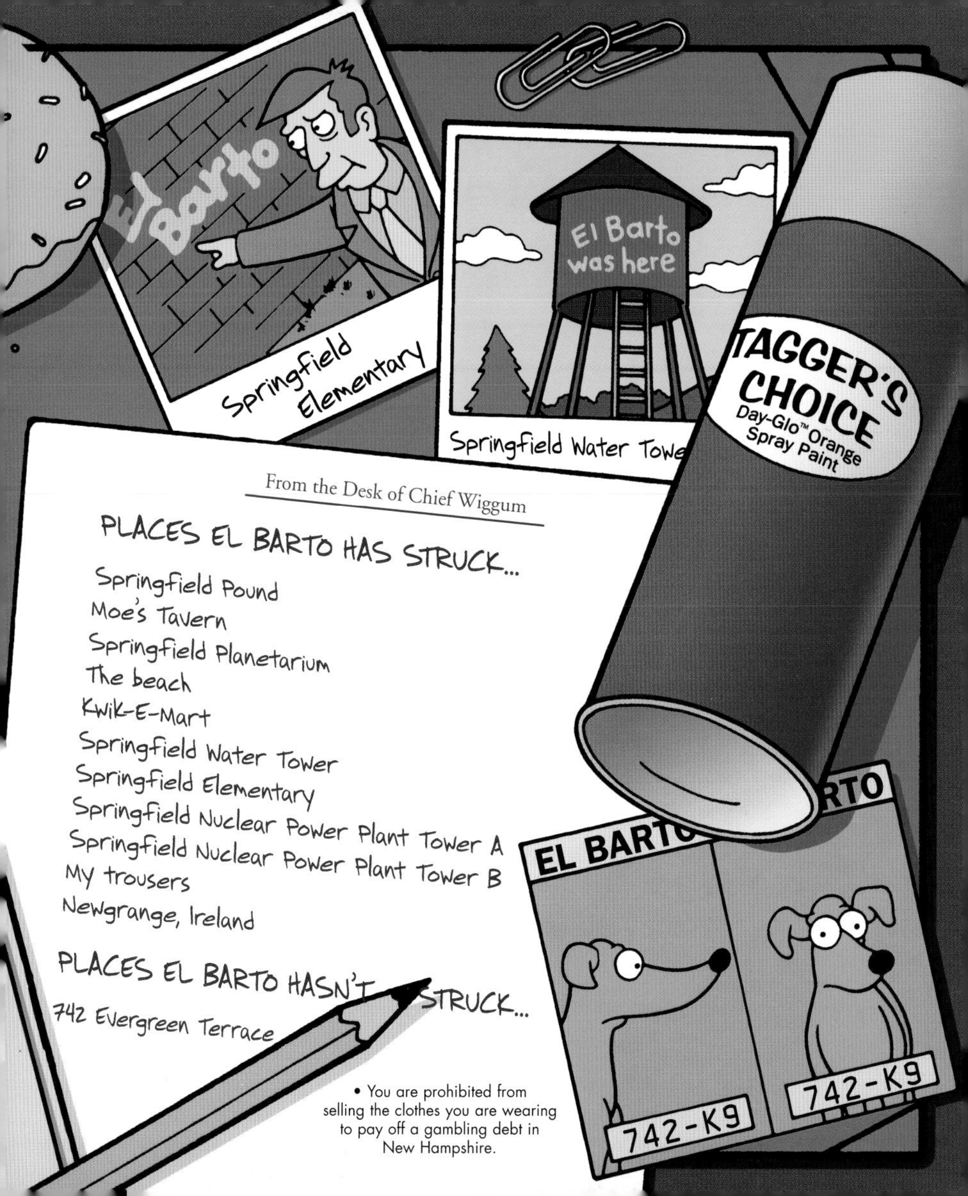
El Barto
Springfield Elementary
El Barto was here
Springfield Water Towe
TAGGER'S CHOICE
Day-Glo™ Orange Spray Paint
From the Desk of Chief Wiggum
PLACES EL BARTO HAS STRUCK...
Springfield Pound
Moe's Tavern
Springfield Planetarium
The beach
Kwik-E-Mart
Springfield Water Tower
Springfield Elementary
Springfield Nuclear Power Plant Tower A
Springfield Nuclear Power Plant Tower B
My trousers
Newgrange, Ireland
PLACES EL BARTO HASN'T STRUCK...
742 Evergreen Terrace
EL BARTO
RTO
742-K9
742-K9

• You are prohibited from selling the clothes you are wearing to pay off a gambling debt in New Hampshire.

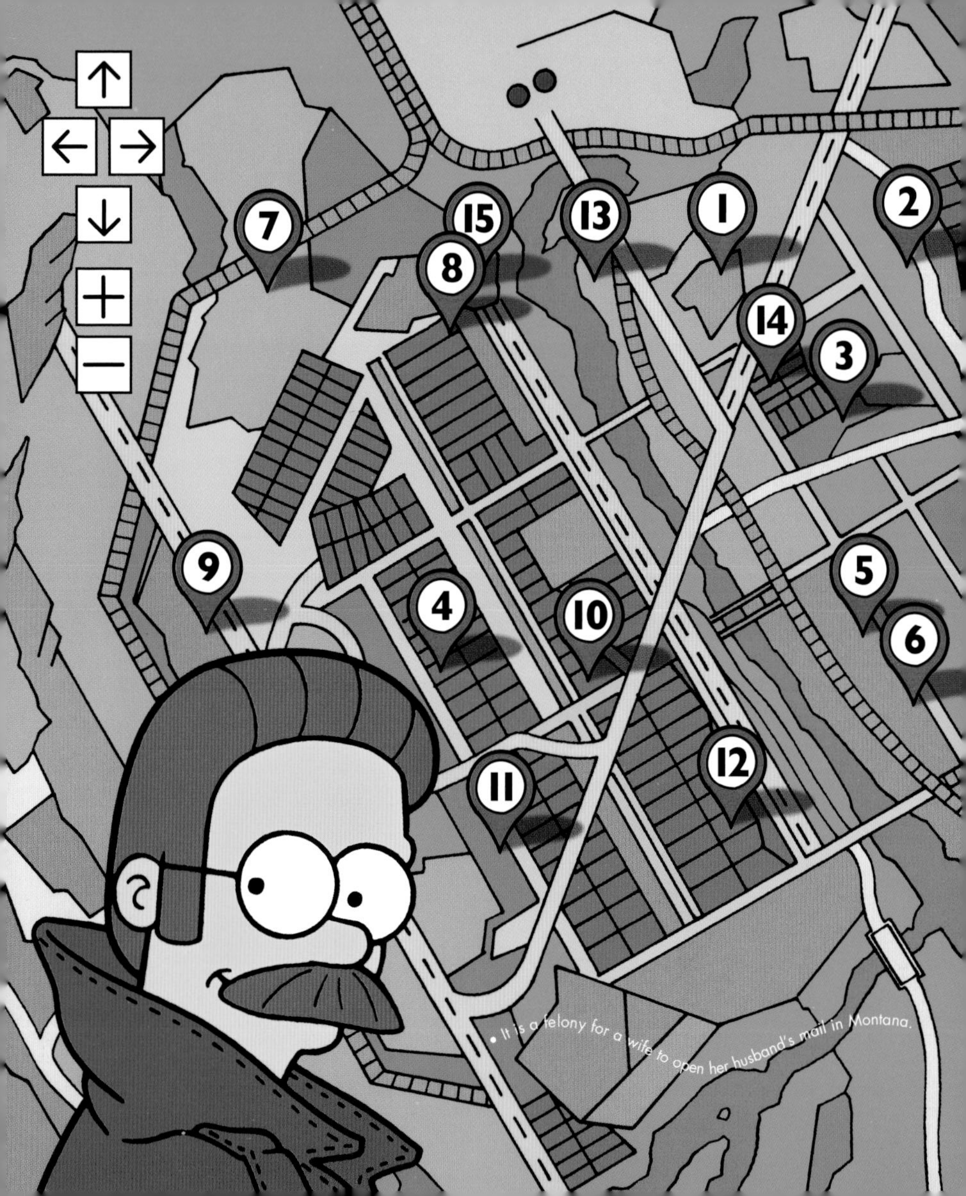
↑
←
→
↓
+
—
7
15
13
1
2
8
14
3
9
4
10
5
6
11
12
• It is a felony for a wife to open her husband's mail in Montana.

Hi-dilly-ho, Neighborinos! I Saw What You Diddily-did!

A LISTING OF REPORTS OF MORAL TURPITUDE IN SPRINGFIELD FROM CITIZEN FLANDERS' NEIGHBORHOOD WATCHEROONIE

RECENT OUTBREAKS OF DEPRAVITY

MONDAY
1. Slight perceived umbrage taken and snit thrown at Miss Tillingham's School for Snooty Girls & Mama's Boys.

TUESDAY
2. Fire Dept. fails to respond to report of "flaming bag of dog-diddily-do" on front porch.

WEDNESDAY
3. Woman of ill repute reputed to be ill after eating at the Tacomat.
4. Koяn played audibly on car stereo in the Try-N-Save parking lot.
5. Police fail to respond to complaint of neighbor's wife being coveted.

THURSDAY
6. Spinster City Apartments resident reported to have been inappropriately touched by an angel.
7. Overtly suggestive merging of traffic observed entering Carter-Nixon Tunnel.
8. Fire Dept. fails to respond to report of "disagreeable odors" emanating from 742 Evergreen Terrace.

FRIDAY
9. Evil-diddily-doers doing evil at the 99¢ Porno Store.
10. Fire Dept. fails to respond to report of a "liar, liar w/ pants on fire" at Moe's Tavern.

SATURDAY
11. Nattering nabobs of negativism overheard emboldening the Enemy at Java the Hut.
12. Satan spotted purchasing fantasy games at Android's Dungeon.
13. Police fail to respond to report of "good time being had by all" at Maison Derrière.

SUNDAY
14. Listener calls in complaint to KBBL about airing ads for Facestuffers' Jumbo Boneless Foot-Long Hot Dogs on the Sabbath.
15. Police fail to disperse crowd gathered to rubberneck during a disgraceful incident at 742 Evergreen Terrace.

THE SPD's LITTLE-KN

10-27p: Going to IHOP on the morning of a police pancake breakfast fund-raiser

10-32c: Wasting precious Cheetos by feeding them to ducks

10-35b: Wearing a baseball cap backward while over the age of 35

10-43a: Calling for backup; officer too full of all-you-can-eat fried shrimp to give chase

10-43b: Officer requesting napkins

10-055: Popping wheelies while driving a school bus

10-112: Interfering with an officer trying to watch "American Idol"

10-116: Tricking an officer into painting a fence by making it appear like "the most fun thing ever"

10-118: Shouting "ba-BOOM, ba-BOOM, ba-BOOM!" when a fat person walks by

10-123: Officer requesting help with remembering which police codes are which

10-220: Making an officer feel "less than"

10-300: Whittling in a library

10-443: Quoting lines from a Will Ferrell movie more than two years after its release

10-449: Impersonating a police horse (front and/or back)

10-545: Making fun of an officer's music selection on the ride back to the station

10-773: Telling an officer to "Chillax"

10-776: Not inviting an officer to "the" barbecue of the summer

10-862: Eating a prizewinning butter statue

OWN POLICE CODES!

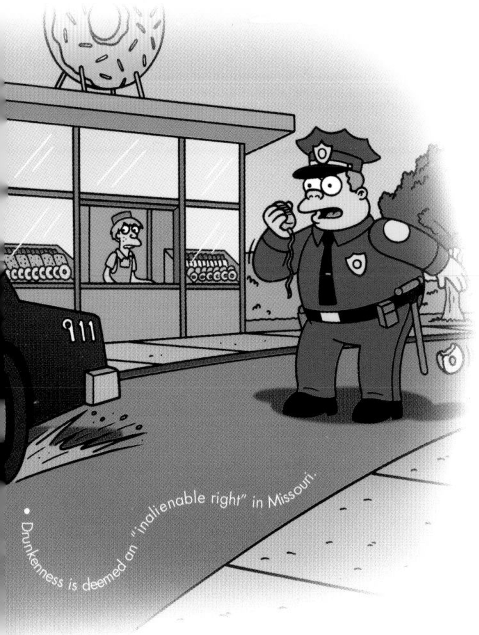
911

• Drunkenness is deemed an "inalienable right" in Missouri.

10-888/FM frequency: Officer immediately requesting the name of the song on the radio

11-223: Looking glum in the presence of a clown

20-009: Failure to cast an officer in a community theater production of "The Fantasticks"

20-807: Forgetting to close the door when using the bathroom

21-555: General shenanigans

21-613: Bogarting an entire plate of free samples

21-743: Leaving the house with a cold

21-836: Falsely claiming your establishment is "Famous for Its Bundt Cake"

21-958: Soup theft

21-958c: Soup theft (offender supplying own container)

22-644: Not holding the onions when specifically asked—TWICE—to hold the onions

22-644f: Not including ketchup packets in a drive-thru order that includes french fries and/or onion rings

22-644k: Spelling ketchup "catsup"

23-111: "Ghost-riding" a Big Wheel

23-127: Arguing about comic book characters in public

23-456: Making an officer believe he has accidentally traveled back in time

23-999: Driving while eating noodles

25-766: Impersonating Hal Holbrook

SPRINGFIELD "LAW AND ORDER" CALENDAR ART

Someone had the bright idea of making a sexy calendar of Springfield's own "Law and Order" cast to raise funds for the Springfield Police Athletic Social Society (SPASS). It worked, when a single, kind citizen bought every copy (to burn them). Unfortunately, one copy survived.

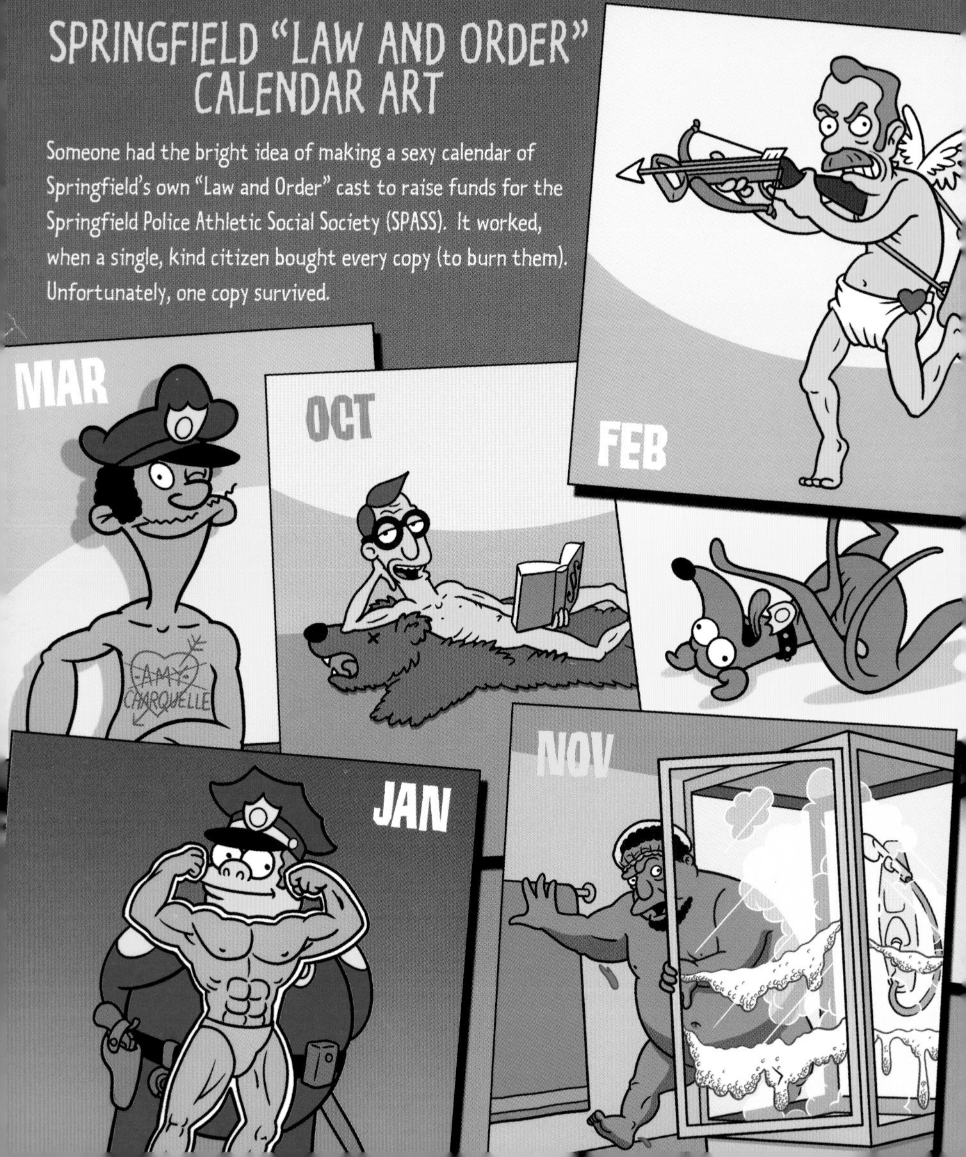

FEB
MAR
AMY
CHARQUELLE
OCT
JAN
NOV

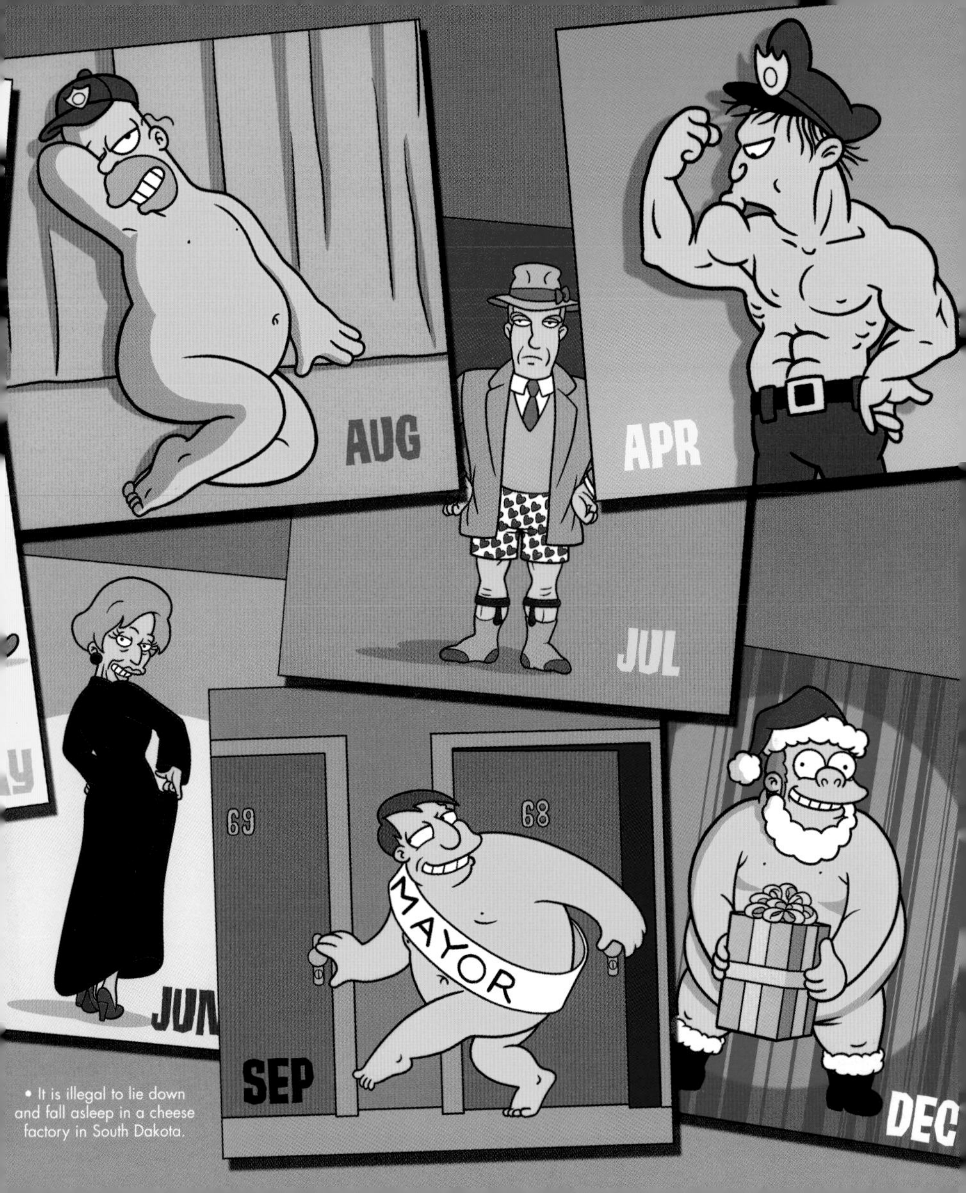
AUG
APR
JUL
JUN
69
68
MAYOR
SEP
DEC

• It is illegal to lie down and fall asleep in a cheese factory in South Dakota.

THE 45 TYPES OF ALLEGED PERPETRATORS YOU MEET ON YOUR BEAT

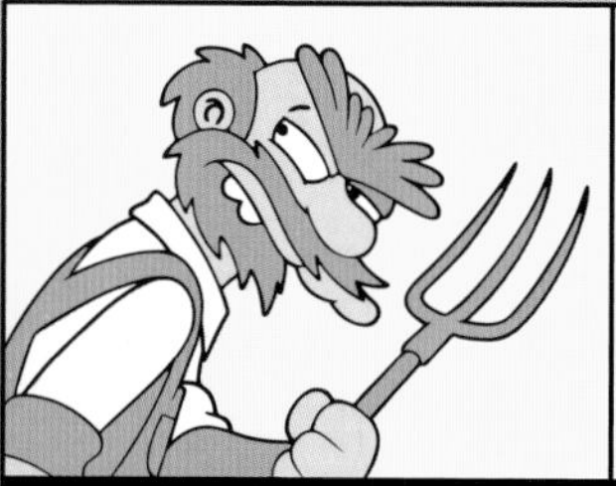
THE HOSTILE WITNESS

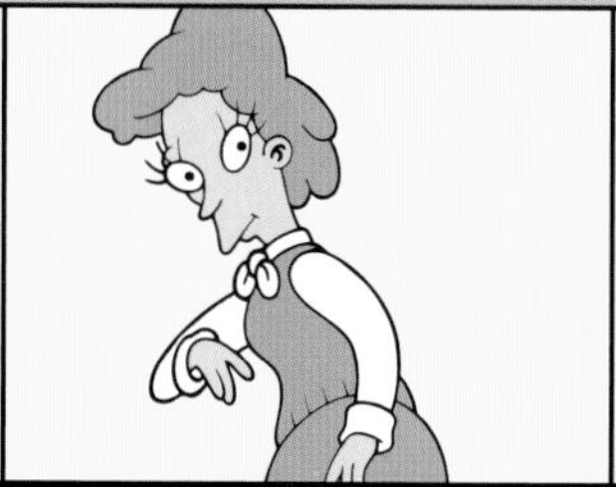
THE BIG BUTTINSKI

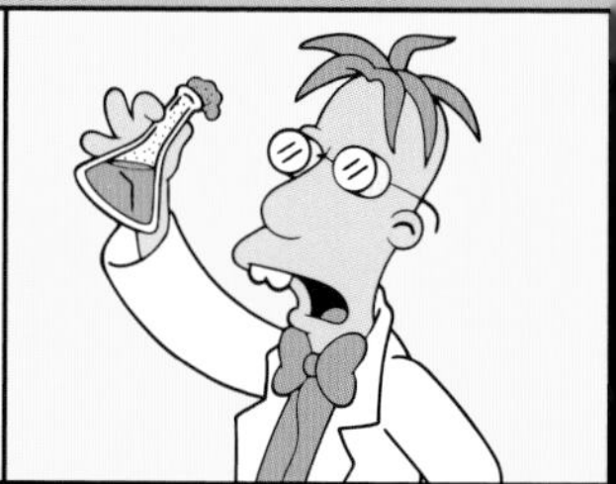
THE MAD PROFESSOR

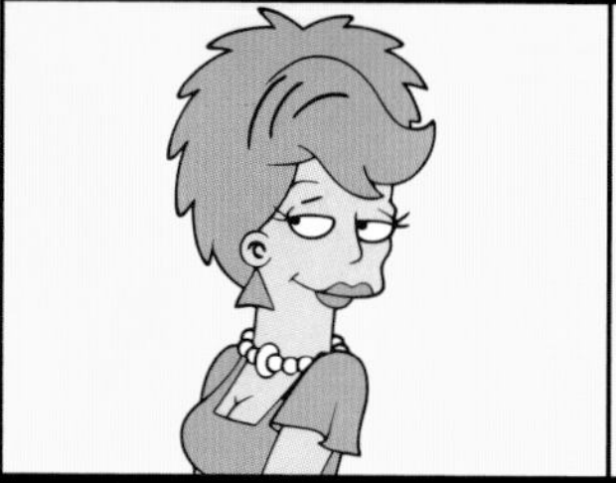
THE FEMME FATALE

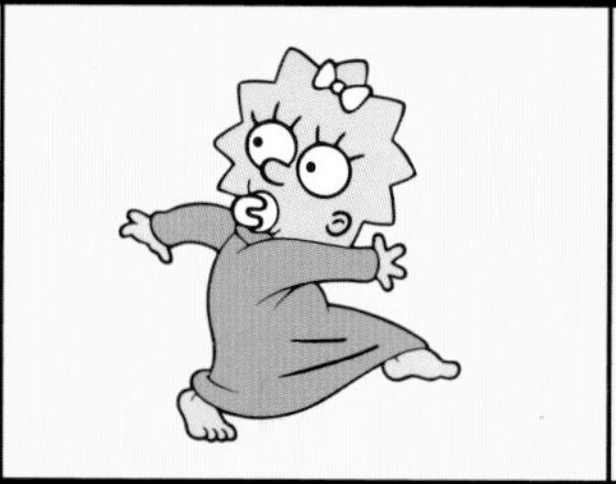
THE ENFANT TERRIBLE

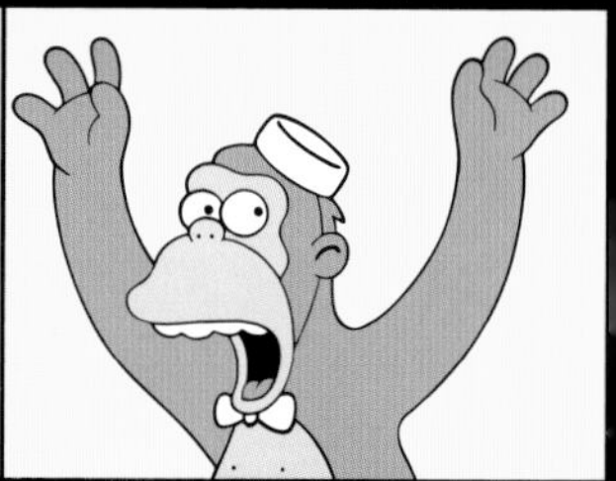
THE FELONIOUS MONK

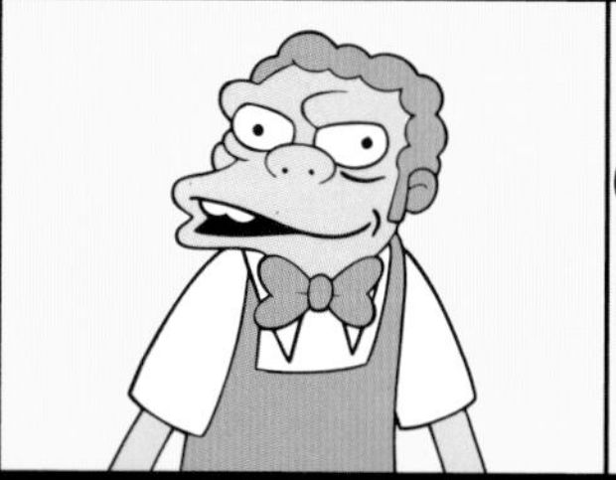
THE BAD APPLE

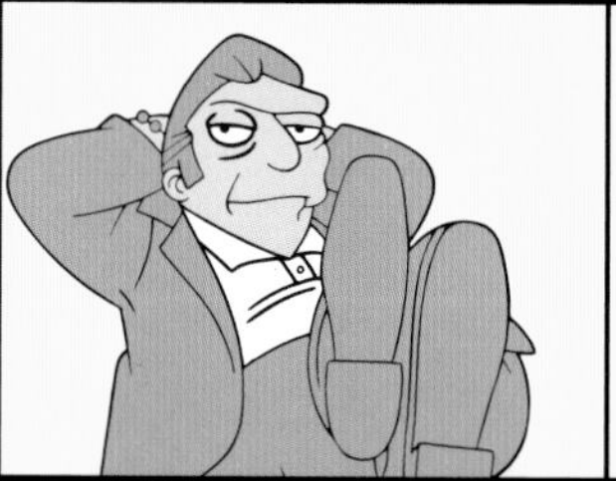
THE "LEGITIMATE BUSINESSMAN"

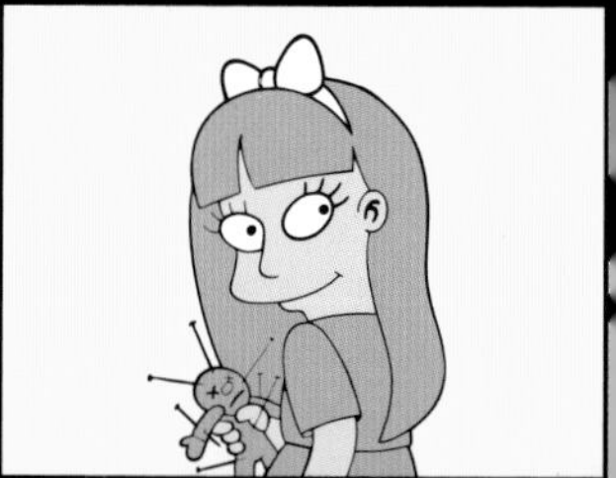
THE LITTLE MISS MISCREANT

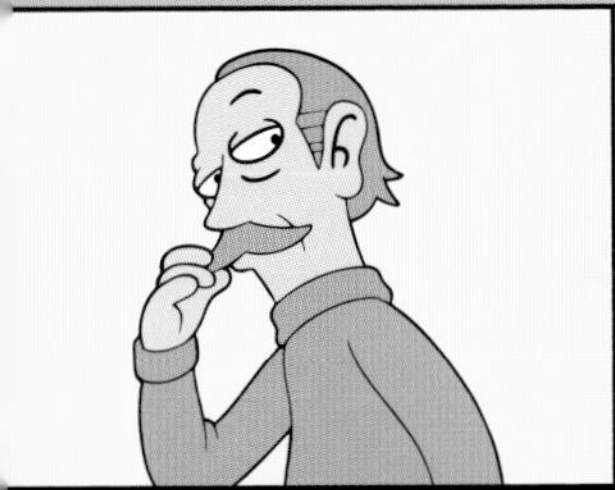
THE CREEPING CAT BURGLAR

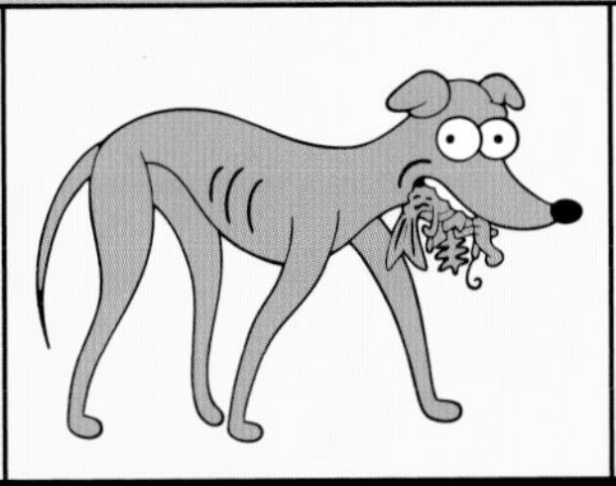
THE LOW-DOWN DIRTY DOG

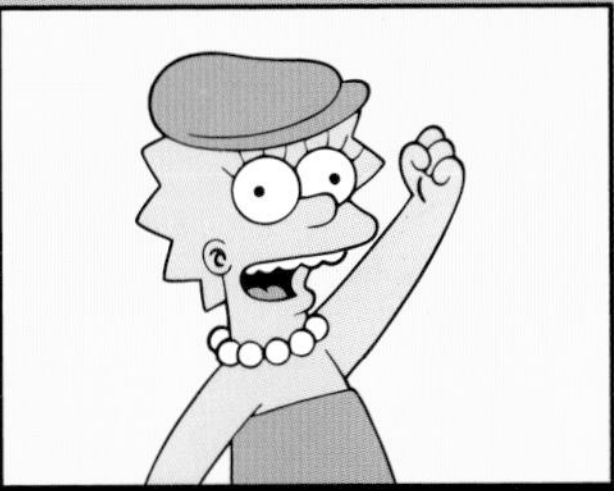
THE RABBLE-ROUSER

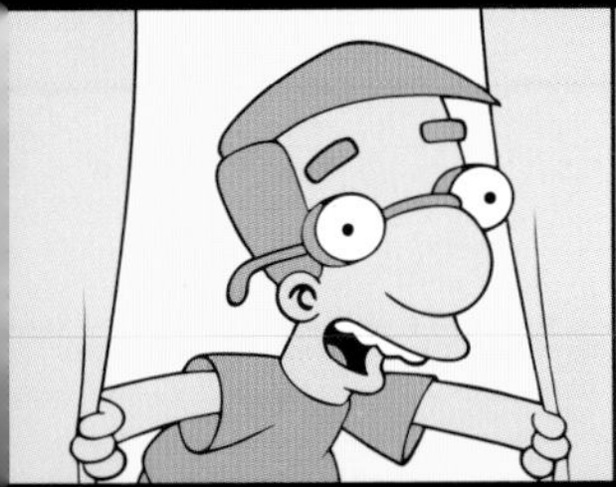
THE CURIOUS ONLOOKER

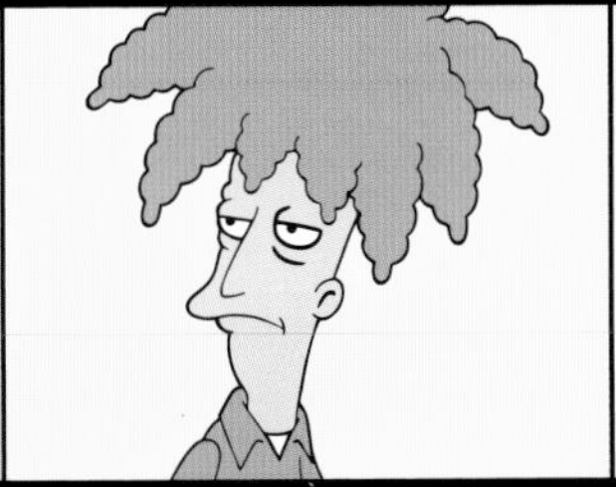
THE GUILTY PARTY

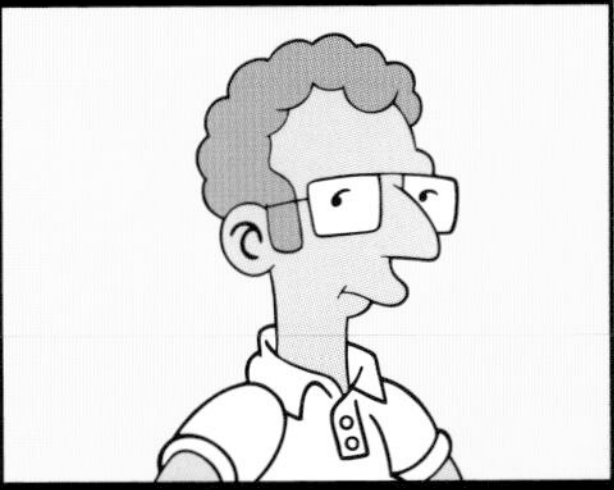
THE NO-GOODNIK

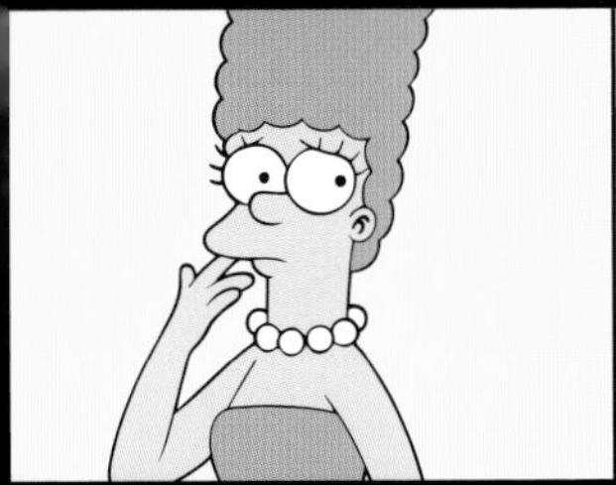
THE INNOCENT BYSTANDER

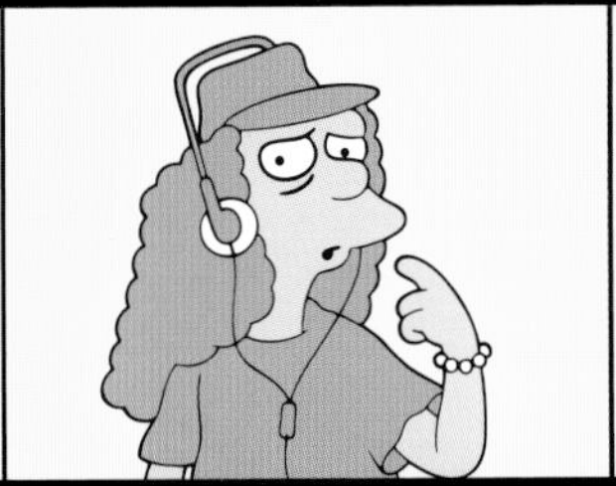
THE PERSON OF INTEREST

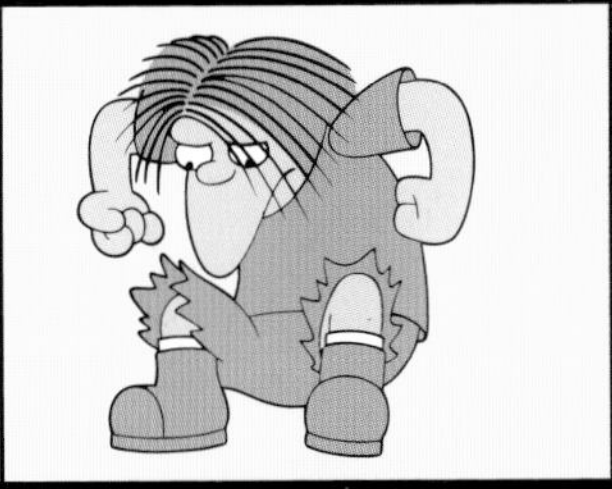
THE LOUSY PUNK KID

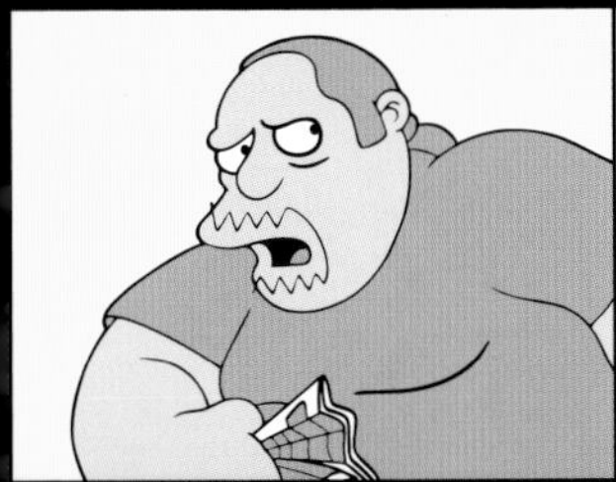
THE MERCHANT OF MENACE

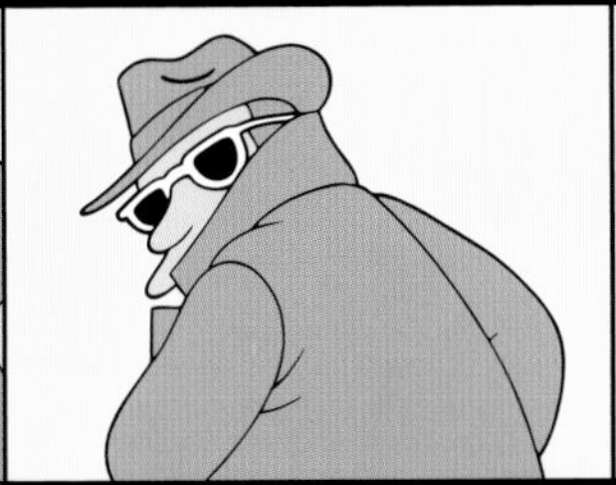
THE STRANGE STRANGER

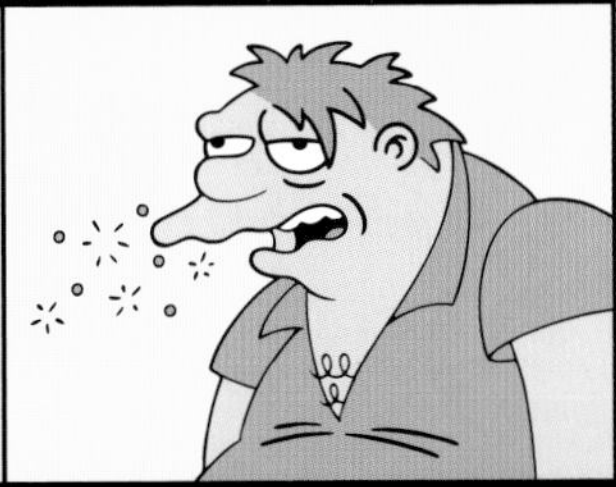
THE SOCIAL MISFIT

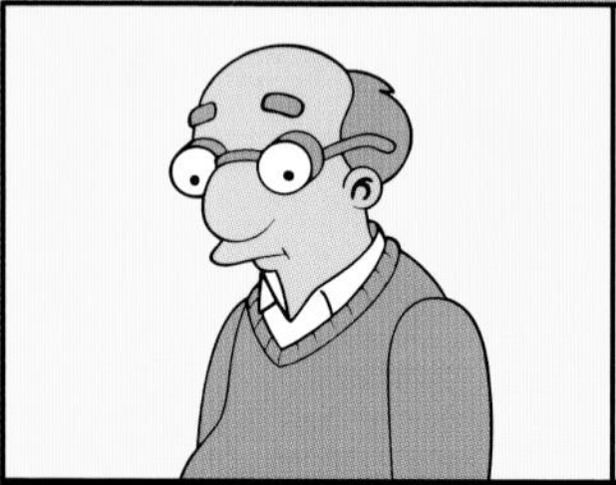

THE NE'ER-DO-WELL

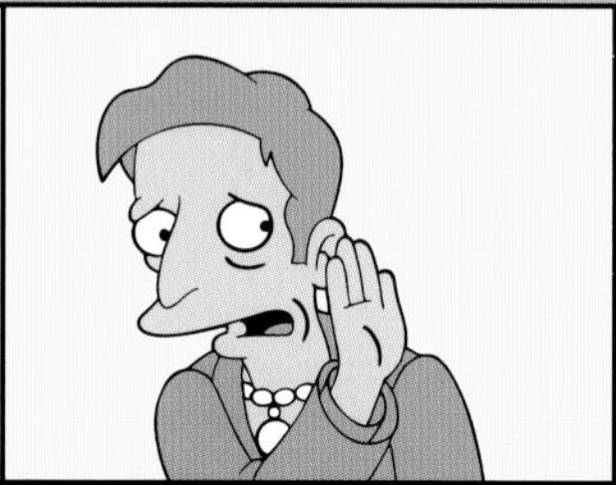

THE STOOL PIGEON

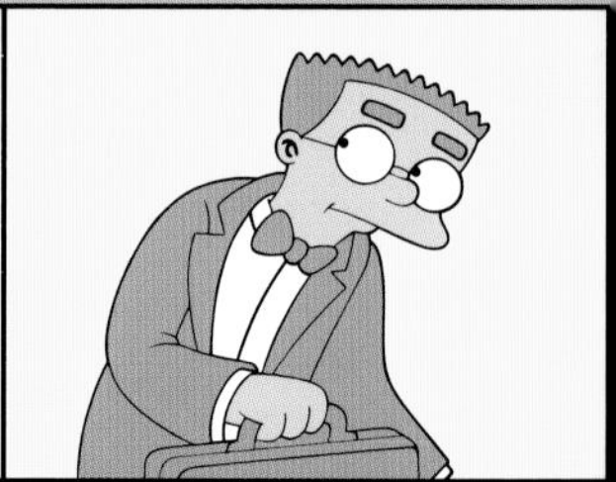

THE ILLEGAL SECRETARY

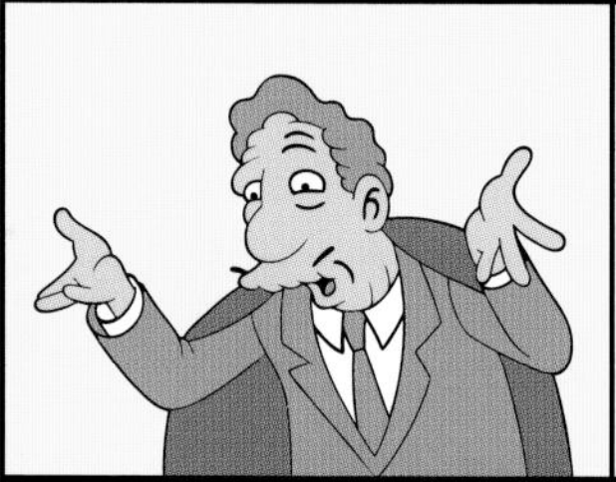

THE LAW BENDER

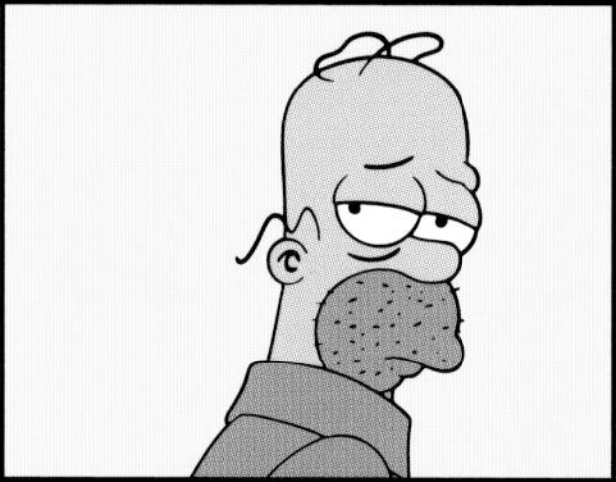

THE DEADBEAT DAD

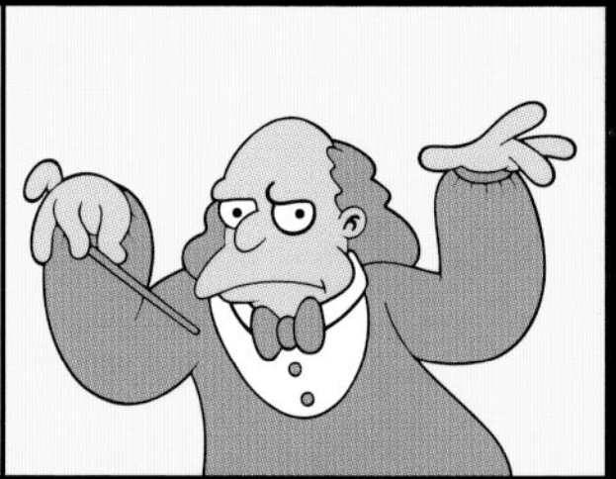

THE DISORDERLY CONDUCTOR

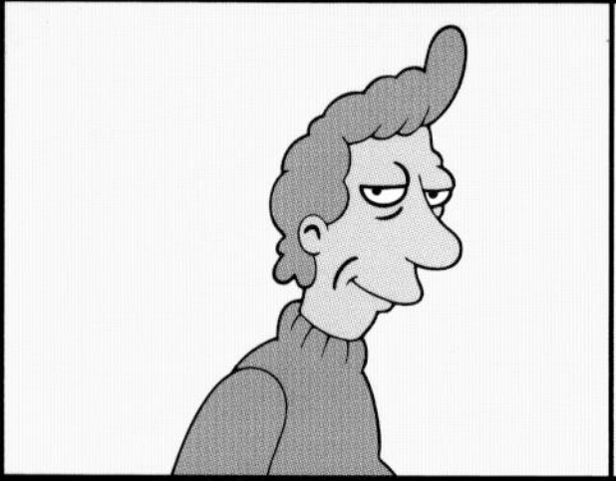

THE FORBIDDEN FRUIT

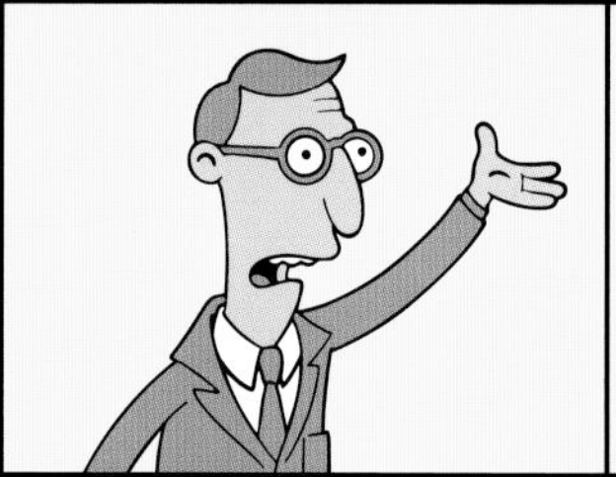

THE CRIMINAL ATTORNEY

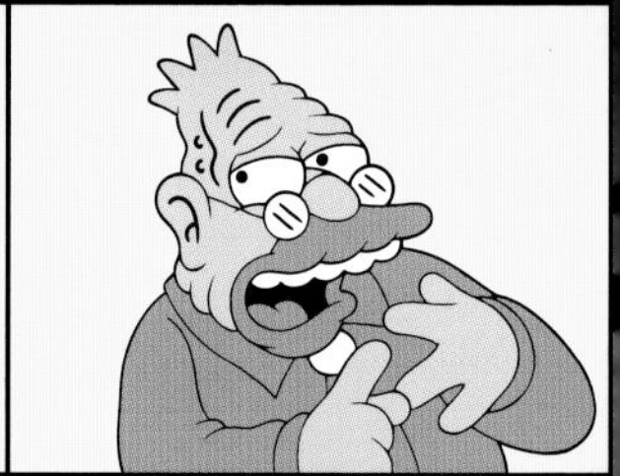

THE PETTIFOGGING HUMBUG

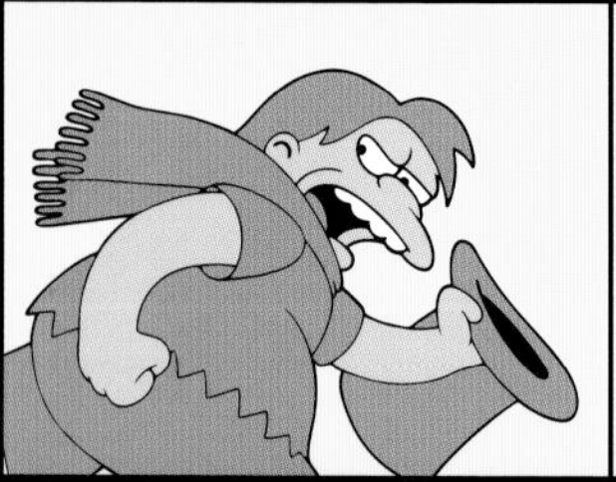

THE LITTLE DICKENS

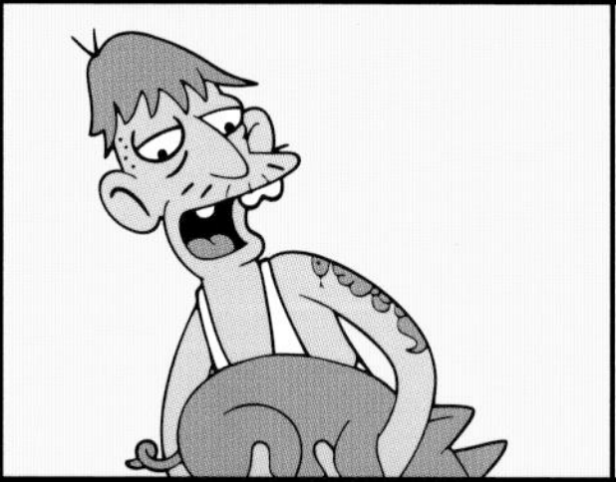

THE RED-HANDED REDNECK

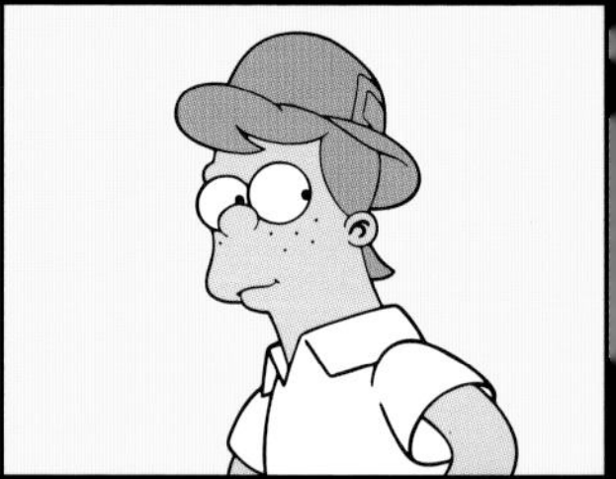

THE ARTFUL DODGER

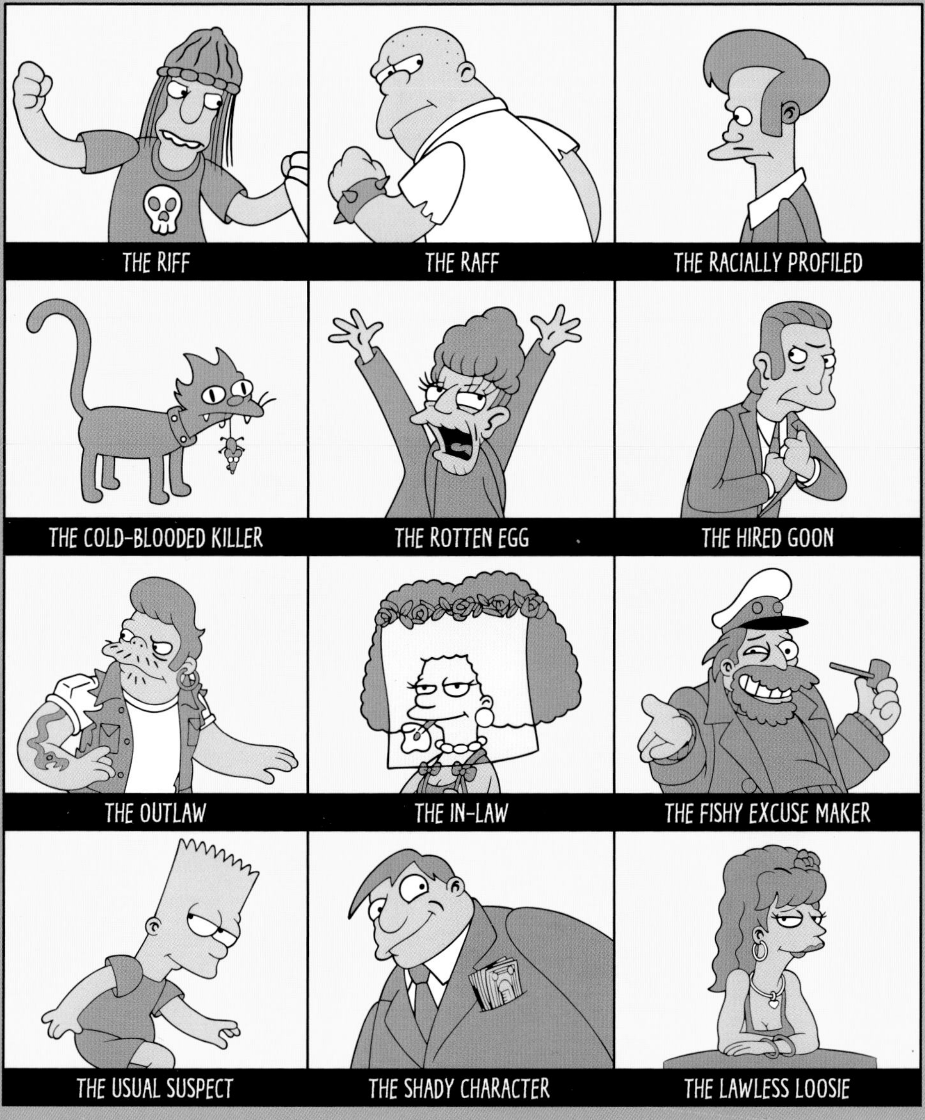
THE RIFF
THE RAFF
THE RACIALLY PROFILED
THE COLD-BLOODED KILLER
THE ROTTEN EGG
THE HIRED GOON
THE OUTLAW
THE IN-LAW
THE FISHY EXCUSE MAKER
THE USUAL SUSPECT
THE SHADY CHARACTER
THE LAWLESS LOOSIE

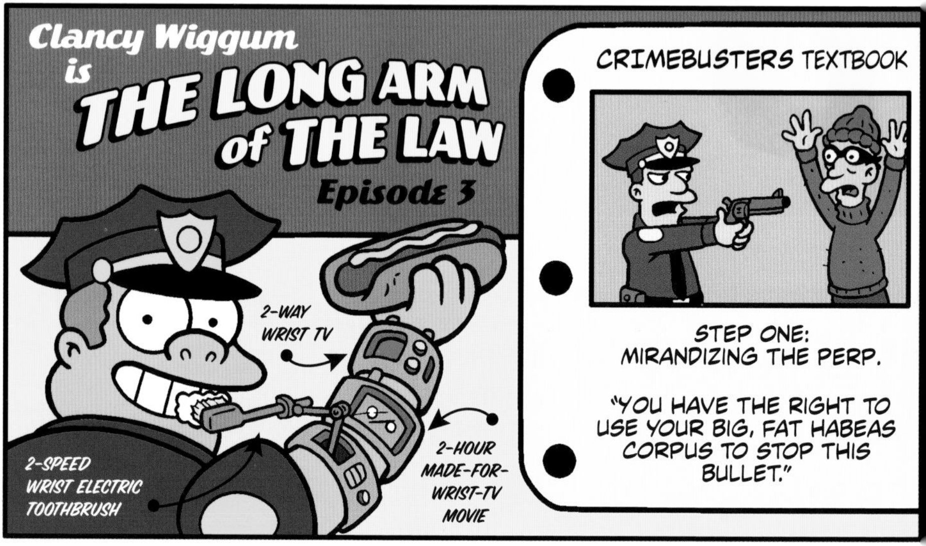
Clancy Wiggum
is
THE LONG ARM of THE LAW
Episode 3
2-WAY WRIST TV
2-SPEED WRIST ELECTRIC TOOTHBRUSH
2-HOUR MADE-FOR-WRIST-TV MOVIE
CRIMEBUSTERS TEXTBOOK
STEP ONE: MIRANDIZING THE PERP.
"YOU HAVE THE RIGHT TO USE YOUR BIG, FAT HABEAS CORPUS TO STOP THIS BULLET."

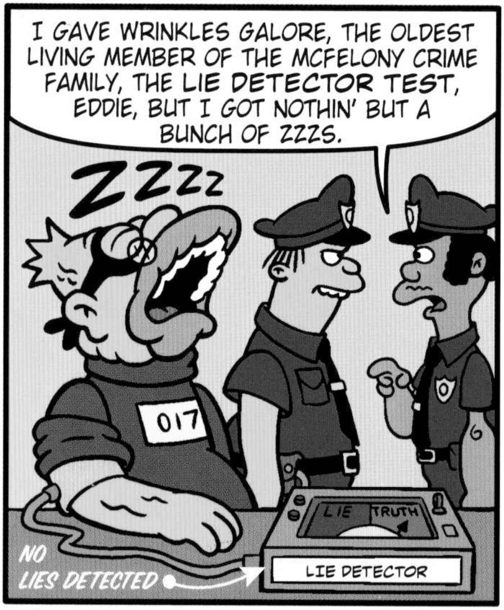
I GAVE WRINKLES GALORE, THE OLDEST LIVING MEMBER OF THE MCFELONY CRIME FAMILY, THE LIE DETECTOR TEST, EDDIE, BUT I GOT NOTHIN' BUT A BUNCH OF ZZZS.
ZZZz
017
LIE
TRUTH
LIE DETECTOR
NO LIES DETECTED

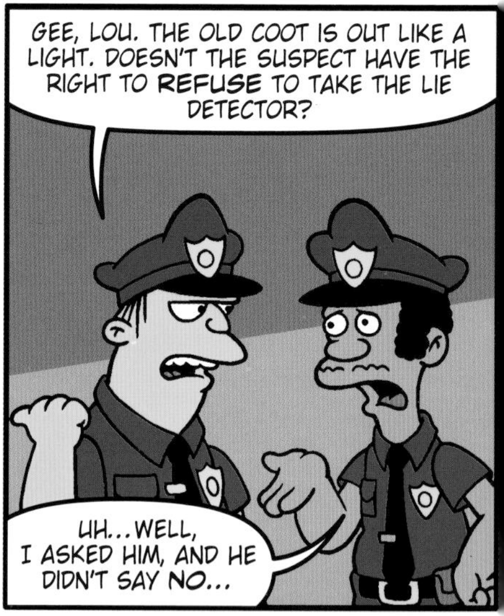
GEE, LOU. THE OLD COOT IS OUT LIKE A LIGHT. DOESN'T THE SUSPECT HAVE THE RIGHT TO REFUSE TO TAKE THE LIE DETECTOR?
UH...WELL, I ASKED HIM, AND HE DIDN'T SAY NO...

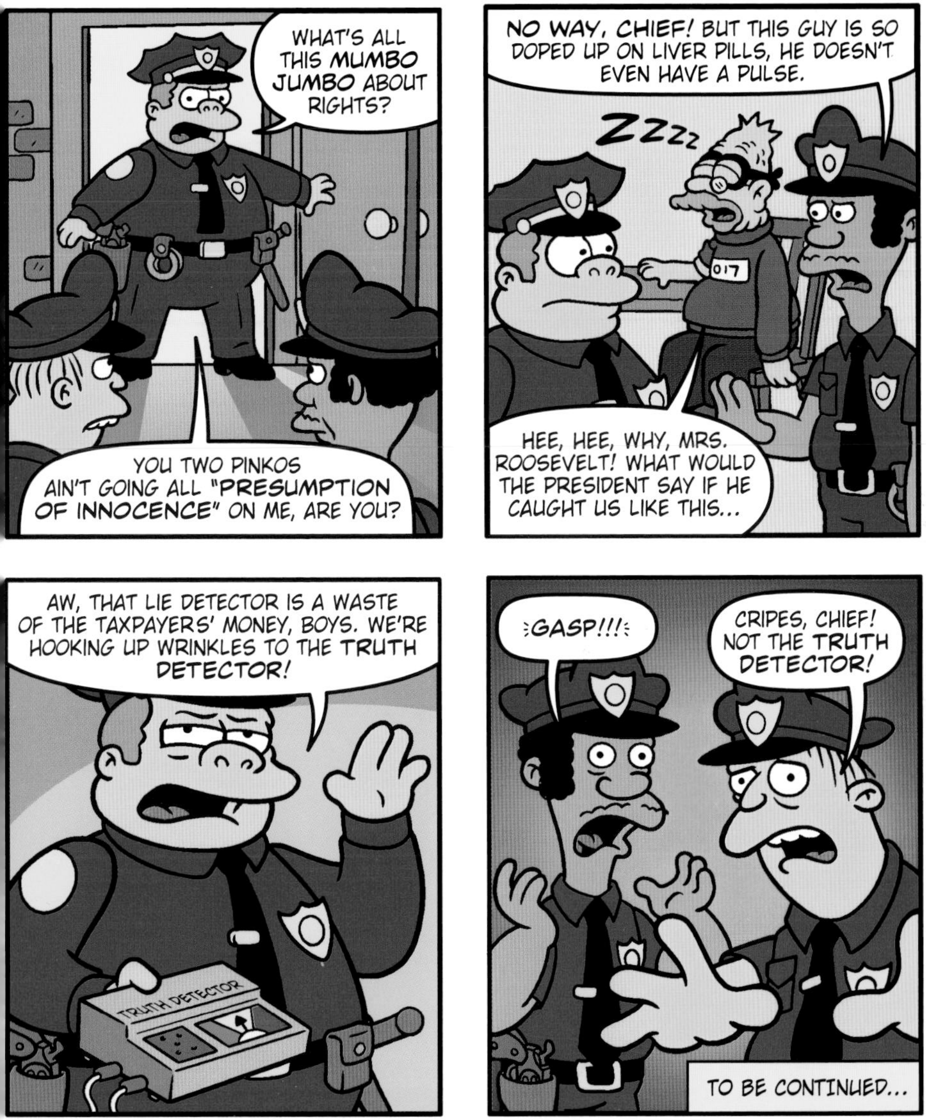
WHAT'S ALL THIS MUMBO JUMBO ABOUT RIGHTS?
YOU TWO PINKOS AIN'T GOING ALL "PRESUMPTION OF INNOCENCE" ON ME, ARE YOU?
NO WAY, CHIEF! BUT THIS GUY IS SO DOPED UP ON LIVER PILLS, HE DOESN'T EVEN HAVE A PULSE.
ZZZZ
017
HEE, HEE, WHY, MRS. ROOSEVELT! WHAT WOULD THE PRESIDENT SAY IF HE CAUGHT US LIKE THIS...
AW, THAT LIE DETECTOR IS A WASTE OF THE TAXPAYERS' MONEY, BOYS. WE'RE HOOKING UP WRINKLES TO THE TRUTH DETECTOR!
TRUTH DETECTOR
GASP!!!
CRIPES, CHIEF! NOT THE TRUTH DETECTOR!
TO BE CONTINUED...

SPRINGFIELD POLICE DEPARTMENT MIRANDA WARNING

Annotated by Clancy Wiggu

- You have the right to remain silent.
  Only read to perps who've never seen a cop show.

- Anything you say can and will be held against you. *If a perp says "Jennifer Lopez" you can beat him with your nightstick.*

- You have the right to have an attorney present during questioning. *Mumble this one and maybe they'll forget you said it.*

- If you cannot afford an attorney, one will be provided for you. *Don't mention that he's probably a night-school dropout.*

- You have the right to moon the judge at your arraignment. *Not really, but saying this increases convictions by 500%.*

- Do you understand the rights I have just read to you? *If "Yes," you got 'em. If "No"...uh, no one ever says "No."*

• In Oklahoma, you are prohibited from taking a bite out of another person's hamburger.

POLICEMAN'S
HANDBOOK

LOADED WITH CHARTS AND GRAPHS TO HELP SPRINGFIELD'S FINEST DO THEIR LEASTEST!

THE LAZY MAN'S GUIDE TO LAW ENFORCEMENT

THE SPRINGFIELD POLICE DEPARTMENT

∼ *Our Vision* ∼
To serve and protect our ass and, if necessary,
our fellow citizens as well.

∼ *Our Promise* ∼
To safeguard the public by limiting the amount of
live ammunition our officers have on hand.

∼ *Our Motto* ∼
If you can't beat them, join them.

THE MIRANDA WARNING

*Regardless of how criminating a suspect may be, he can't
incriminate himself unless he is advised of his Miranda rights.
We think the name comes from Carmen Miranda, the lady in the
big tutti-frutti hat in those old movies, but we're not sure.
Anyhow, don't bother memorizing it, just cut along the
dotted lines and paste the following inside your hat.*

✂

"You have the right to say anything that can and will be
used against you in a court of law. You have the right to hire a competent
attorney. If you cannot afford one, an incompetent one will be provided for
you at no cost or obligation. We accept no liability for bruises, contusions,
loss of dignity, or spilled drinks caused by the arresting officer.
Thank you and have a nice day."

PROPER USE OF THE TERM "ALLEGED"

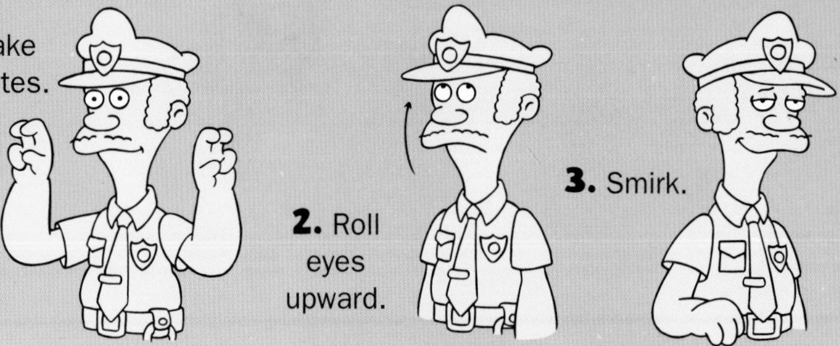

1. Make air quotes.

2. Roll eyes upward.

3. Smirk.

THE 3 TYPES OF DOMESTIC DISTURBANCES

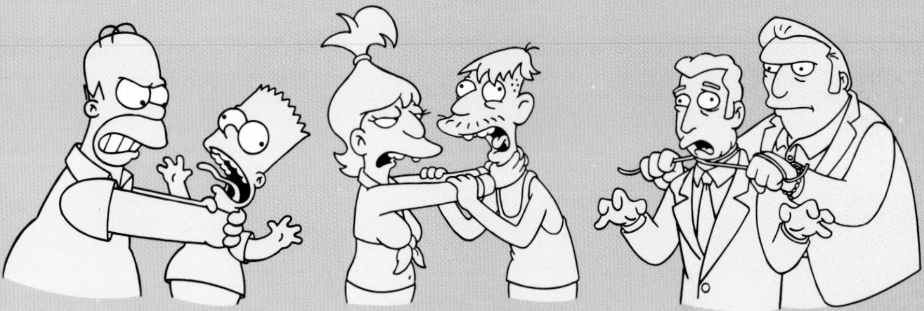

1. Family squabble.

2. Family feud.

3. Family business.

THE 3 TYPES OF DRUNK DRIVERS

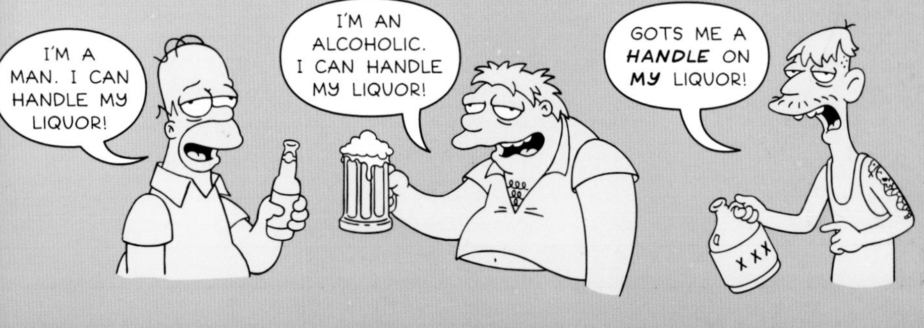
I'M A MAN. I CAN HANDLE MY LIQUOR!
I'M AN ALCOHOLIC. I CAN HANDLE MY LIQUOR!
GOTS ME A ***HANDLE*** ON ***MY*** LIQUOR!
XXX

The Springfield Unorganized Crime Undercover Patrol (commonly referred to as SUCUP) was created to organize miscellaneous crimes into this user-friendly pie-chart configuration and to show their prevalence in the overall picture of crime in Springfield.

UNORGANIZED CRIME CHART

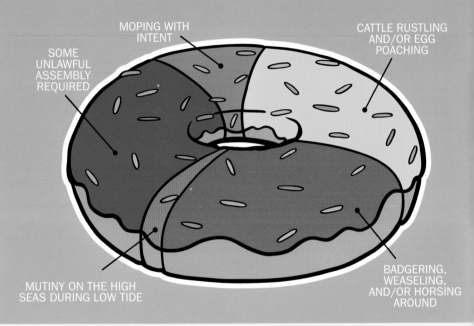

MOPING WITH INTENT

CATTLE RUSTLING AND/OR EGG POACHING

SOME UNLAWFUL ASSEMBLY REQUIRED

MUTINY ON THE HIGH SEAS DURING LOW TIDE

BADGERING, WEASELING, AND/OR HORSING AROUND

COP TALK

GLOSSARY OF POLICE TERMS, ACRONYMS, AND JARGON

APB - All Peanut Butter/No Jelly.
DUI - Do Utmost to Ignore.
DWI - Disregard Wiggum's Instructions.
Officer Down - Cop has fallen and can't get up.
Felony - How the fallen officer landed.
Back Up - Fallen officer okay/standing.
Drop a Dime - Put money in tip jar.

Mug Shot - Fast swig of coffee.
Code One - Temperatures in the low 40s.
Stakeout - Let's order this to go.
LOL - Look Out, Lou!
Juvie - Like, way immature.
Manslaughter - Macho guffaw.
Habeas Corpus - Dead guy.

POLICE SKETCH ARTISTS!

*TIRED OF SKETCHING THE SAME FACES OVER AND OVER?
SAY "GOOD RIDDANCE, OUTDATED PAPER AND PENCILS!"
TO YOUR OUTDATED PAPER AND PENCILS—WITH THE NEW*
PERP-O-MATIC® COMPOSITE GENERATOR.
*YOU'LL HAVE EYEWITNESSES SHOUTING "THAT'S HIM!"
WITH JUST A CLICK OF THE MOUSE!*

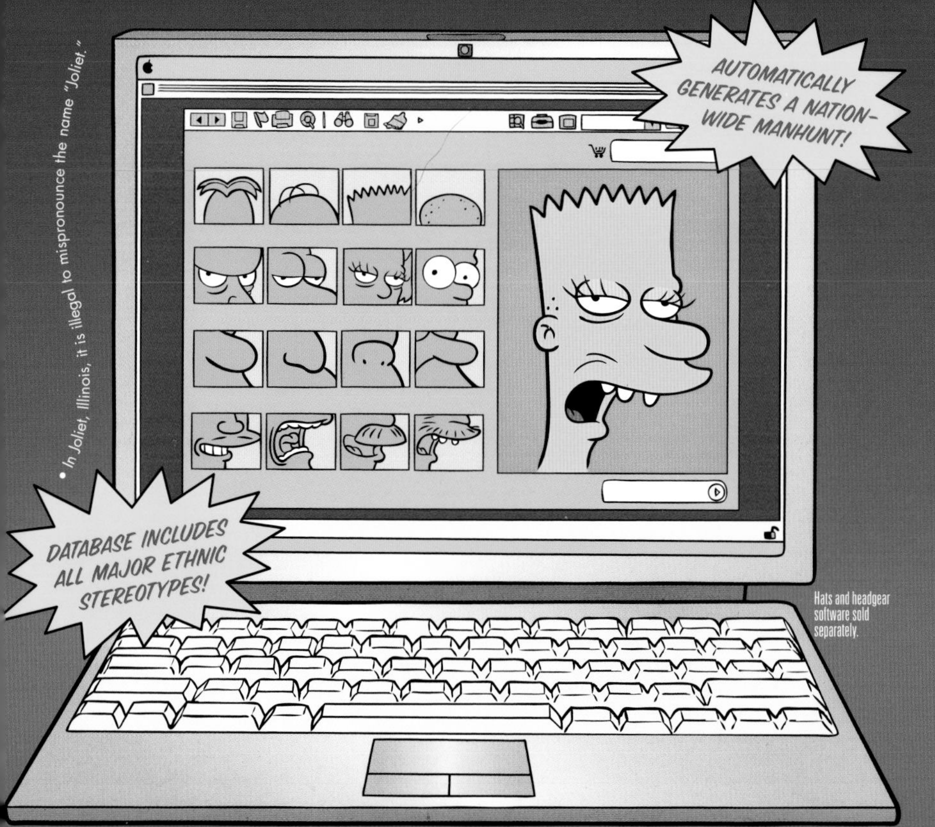
AUTOMATICALLY GENERATES A NATION-WIDE MANHUNT!
DATABASE INCLUDES ALL MAJOR ETHNIC STEREOTYPES!

Hats and headgear software sold separately.

• In Joliet, Illinois, it is illegal to mispronounce the name "Joliet."

OTHER BOOKS YOU MAY ENJOY FROM OUR
LAZY MAN'S LIBRARY

THE LAZY MAN'S GUIDE TO NEUROSURGERY
THE LAZY MAN'S GUIDE TO AIR TRAFFIC CONTROL
THE LAZY MAN'S GUIDE TO STRUCTURAL ENGINEERING
THE LAZY MAN'S GUIDE TO HOMELAND SECURITY
THE LAZY MAN'S GUIDE TO WRITING LAZY MAN'S GUIDES

LAZY MAN'S LIBRARY Published by **Snoozin & Loozin**

• No person may own more than two adult cats in Bartlesville, Oklahoma.

SPRINGFIELD POLICE
Basic Rates in Buying Exemptions Guide
(B.R.I.B.E.s)
To be collected immediately upon notice of violation

Civil Code Infractions

Business Code: 40 percent of cost of correction paid to "Widows and Orphans Fund."
Health Code: Dinner for two (Nov. 20 to Dec. 24: One turkey or goose).
Liquor License: Unlimited well drinks. Call brands require added gratuity.
Public Safety or Fire Code: Free admission into concert or theater venue.

Traffic Violations

Pedestrian: Officer's choice of watch, designer outerwear, or handheld electronics.
Parking: Donation to "Civic Pride Week" of at least 50 percent of ticket penalty.
Moving: Cash only (see chart on back of Springfield driver's license).

Misdemeanors

Class A (Victimless Crimes): 20 Policemen's Ball tickets.
Class C (Contraband Crimes): Case of good Scotch or box of imported cigars.
Class S (Bookmaking Crimes): 20 percent per week.

Felonies

White-Collar: 100 shares of preferred stock in offshore account.
Armed: 2 percent of take for every letter in name of crime.
Bodily Injury: Weight of victim in Krugerrands.
Murder: Market price.

Internal Affairs Investigations

Quotes available on request.

STOP AND WE'LL SHOOT!

Eddie & Lou's Album of Crime-Scene Photos

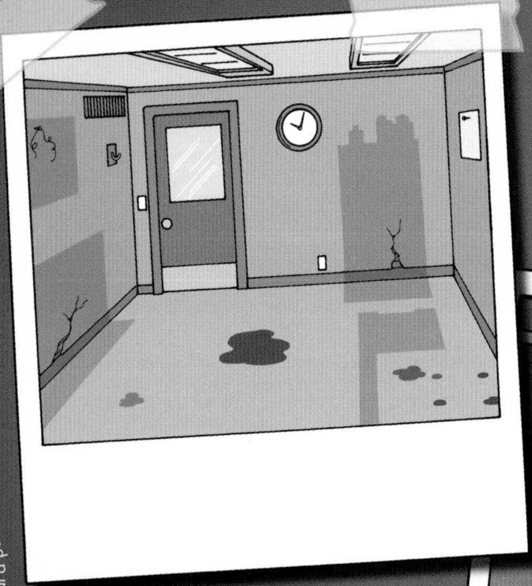

Principal Skinner reported that his office had been stolen. However, when we arrived on the scene, the office was still there. So we booked him for filing a false report.

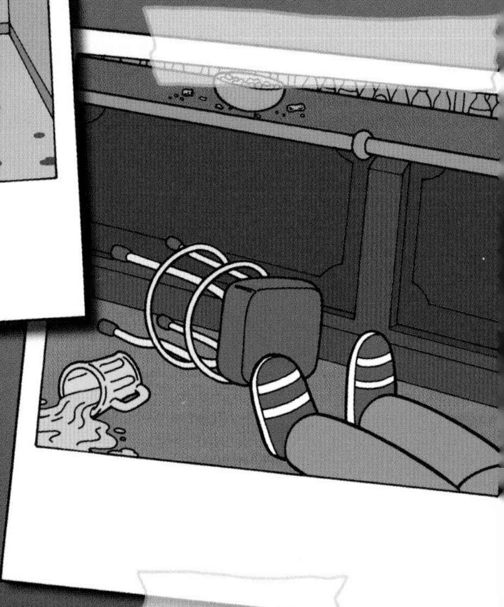

The ol' Gumble stumble and tumble! Friday night in Springfield ain't over till we get our "Man down at Moe's!" call on the radio.

• In Kentucky, it's the law that a person must take a bath once a year.

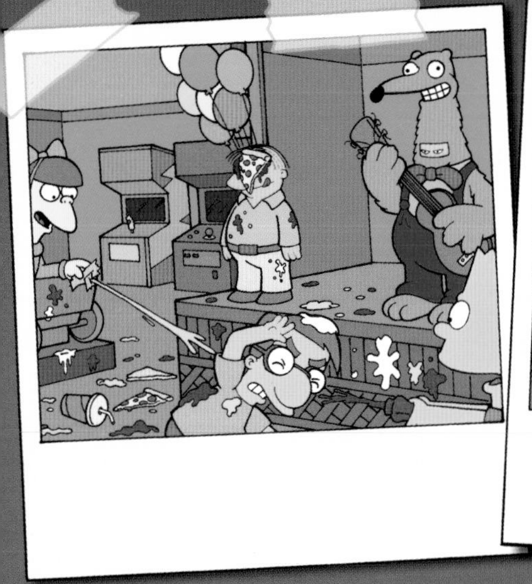

Call in the S.P.L.A.T.* team! Food fight in progress at Wall E. Weasel's.

*Slimy Projectiles Logistics and Tactics

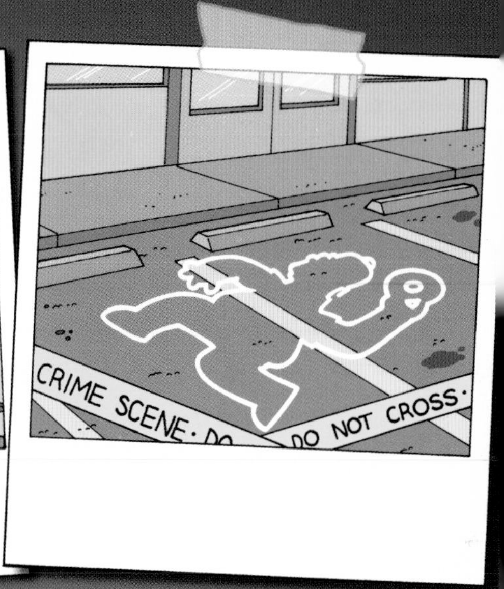

CRIME SCENE · DO
DO NOT CROSS ·

This was another "Man down" call we got...this time at the Kwik-E-Mart parking lot. The man stayed down long enough for us to draw a chalk outline around him and then he got up and left.

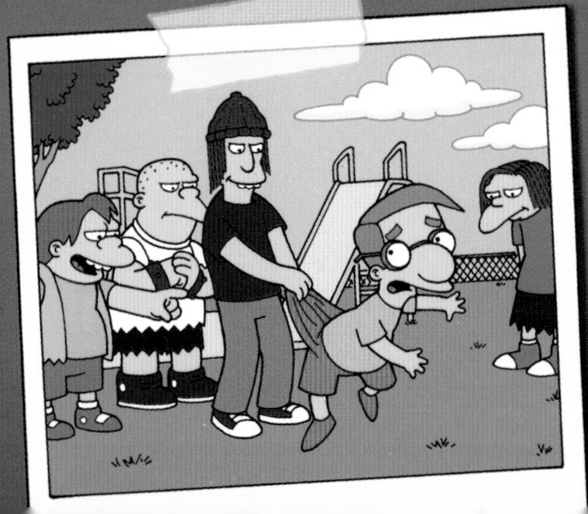

There's no police code for "aggravated wedgie"...but there oughta be!

A steaming bag of dog doo-doo was set on fire and left on the doorstep of the Flanders house. DNA samples sent to the crime lab indicate some type of small gray racing hound.

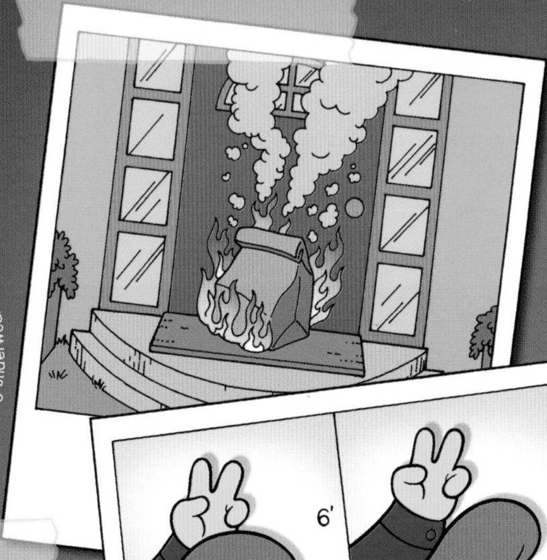

• In Thailand, it is illegal to leave your house if you are not wearing underwear.

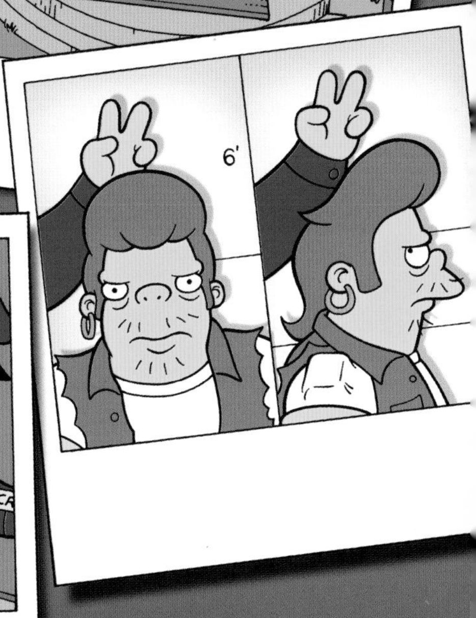
6'

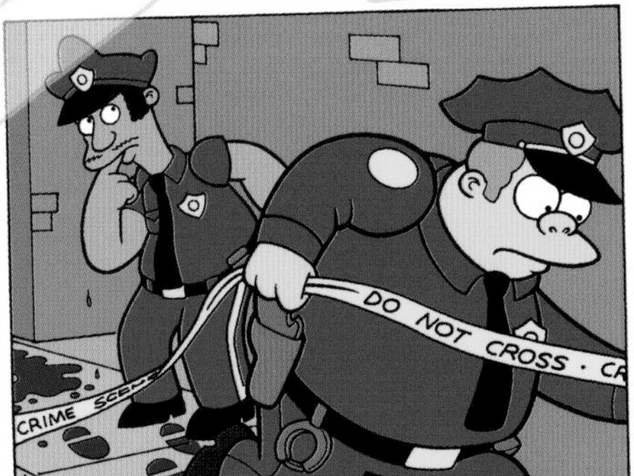
DO NOT CROSS
CRIME

POLICE PROCEDURE BY THE BOOK!

Lou checks to see if that red gooey stuff is paint or real live blood, while the chief secures the crime scene.

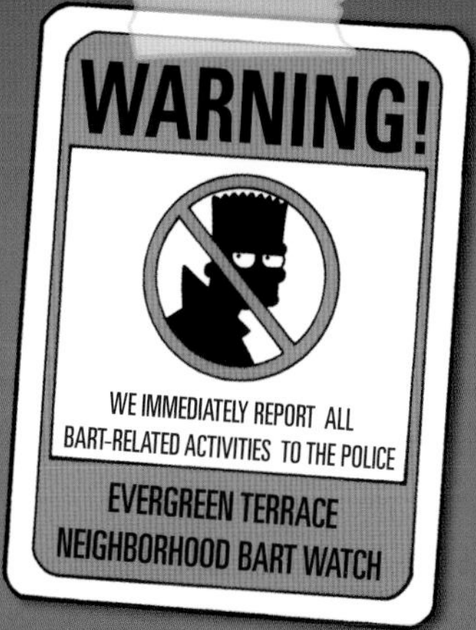
WARNING!
WE IMMEDIATELY REPORT ALL BART-RELATED ACTIVITIES TO THE POLICE
EVERGREEN TERRACE NEIGHBORHOOD BART WATCH

We posted over a dozen of these neighborhood watch signs. They were all stolen within a week.

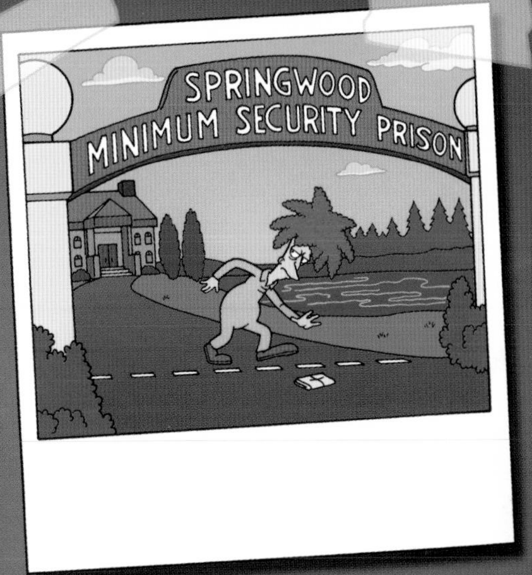
SPRINGWOOD MINIMUM SECURITY PRISON

We got a call reporting a convict attempting to escape from the Springwood Minimum Security Prison...Turns out he was just stepping out to the driveway to pick up his copy of the "Walled-In Journal."

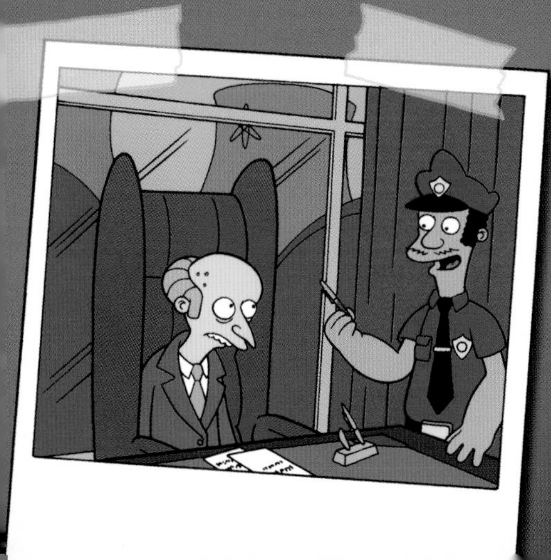

Another case solved by sharp police detective work! After responding to a code five-niner (missing fountain pen) at Mr. Burns' office, Lou quickly detected that the pen had rolled off the desk and onto the floor.

CLANCY PANTS

THE LAWMEN'S-WEAR CLOTHING CATALOGUE

LAW-ENFORCEMENT UNIFORMS MAKE THE MAN "THE MAN"...AND NOTHING SAYS "SIR, PUT YOUR HANDS WHERE I CAN SEE THEM! LIE FACEDOWN ON YOUR STOMACH AND SPREAD YOUR LEGS!" LIKE A SHARP, WELL-PRESSED UNIFORM.

Going undercover can be deadly, especially if your fellow cops don't recognize you immediately as an undercover cop. That's why we never take to the streets without our

REGULATION UNDERCOVER VICE COP ENSEMBLE

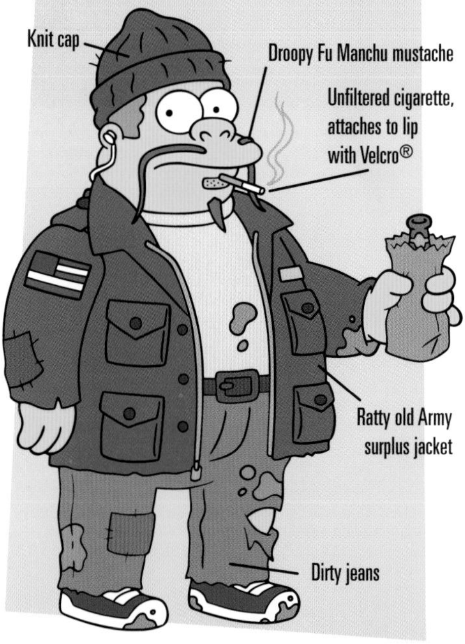

Knit cap
Droopy Fu Manchu mustache
Unfiltered cigarette, attaches to lip with Velcro®
Ratty old Army surplus jacket
Dirty jeans

What better way to convey a feeling of security to shoppers than with a high-school dropout wearing a police-type uniform and carrying a gun?

MONSTRO MART SECURITY GUARD COSTUME

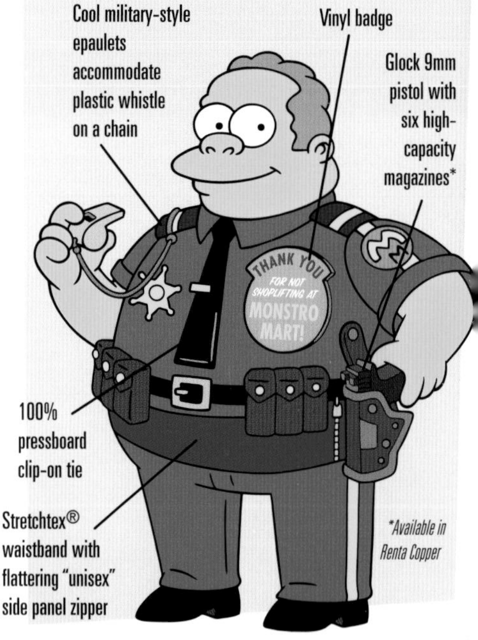

Cool military-style epaulets accommodate plastic whistle on a chain
Vinyl badge
THANK YOU FOR NOT SHOPLIFTING AT MONSTRO MART!
Glock 9mm pistol with six high-capacity magazines*
100% pressboard clip-on tie
Stretchtex® waistband with flattering "unisex" side panel zipper

*Available in Renta Copper

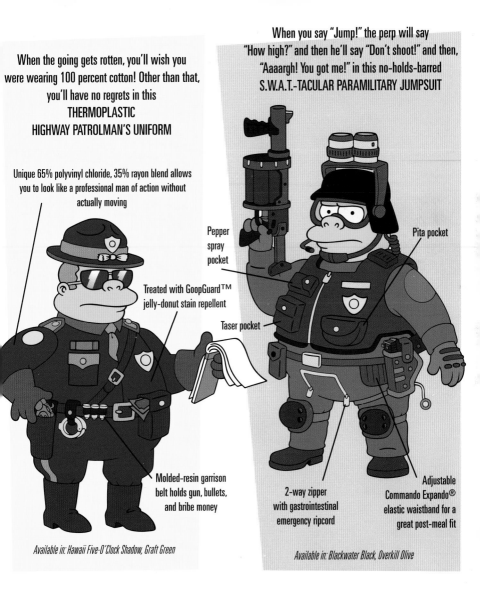

When the going gets rotten, you'll wish you were wearing 100 percent cotton! Other than that, you'll have no regrets in this

THERMOPLASTIC HIGHWAY PATROLMAN'S UNIFORM

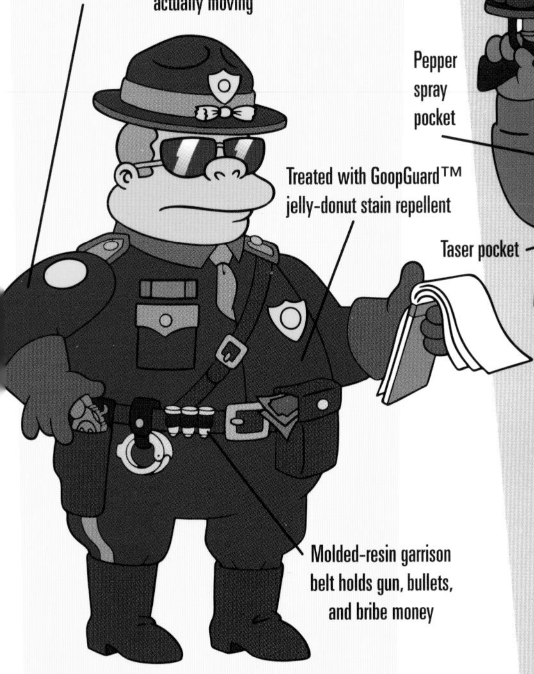
Unique 65% polyvinyl chloride, 35% rayon blend allows you to look like a professional man of action without actually moving
Treated with GoopGuard™ jelly-donut stain repellent
Molded-resin garrison belt holds gun, bullets, and bribe money

Available in: Hawaii Five-O'Clock Shadow, Graft Green

When you say "Jump!" the perp will say "How high?" and then he'll say "Don't shoot!" and then, "Aaaargh! You got me!" in this no-holds-barred

S.W.A.T.-TACULAR PARAMILITARY JUMPSUIT

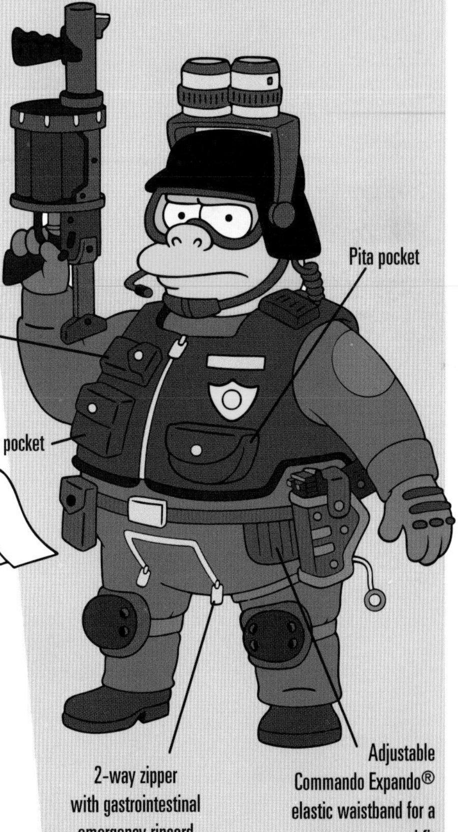
Pepper spray pocket
Pita pocket
Taser pocket
2-way zipper with gastrointestinal emergency ripcord
Adjustable Commando Expando® elastic waistband for a great post-meal fit

Available in: Blackwater Black, Overkill Olive

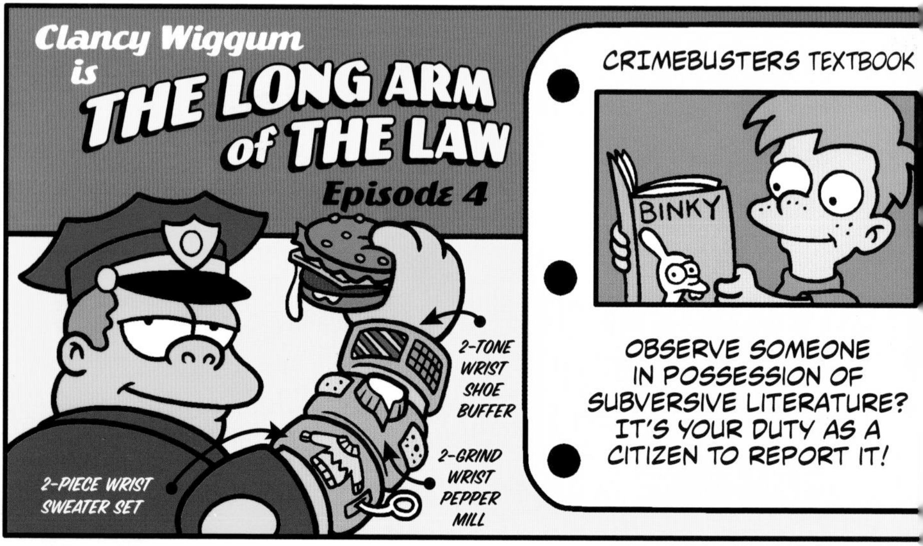
Clancy Wiggum is
THE LONG ARM of THE LAW
Episode 4
2-TONE WRIST SHOE BUFFER
2-GRIND WRIST PEPPER MILL
2-PIECE WRIST SWEATER SET
CRIMEBUSTERS TEXTBOOK
BINKY
OBSERVE SOMEONE IN POSSESSION OF SUBVERSIVE LITERATURE? IT'S YOUR DUTY AS A CITIZEN TO REPORT IT!

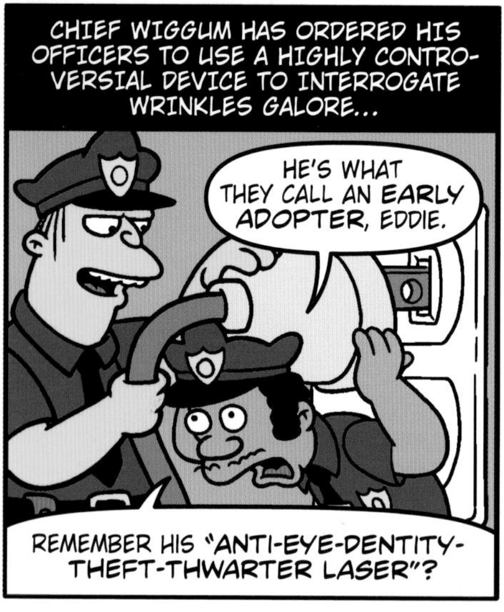
CHIEF WIGGUM HAS ORDERED HIS OFFICERS TO USE A HIGHLY CONTROVERSIAL DEVICE TO INTERROGATE WRINKLES GALORE...
HE'S WHAT THEY CALL AN EARLY ADOPTER, EDDIE.
REMEMBER HIS "ANTI-EYE-DENTITY-THEFT-THWARTER LASER"?

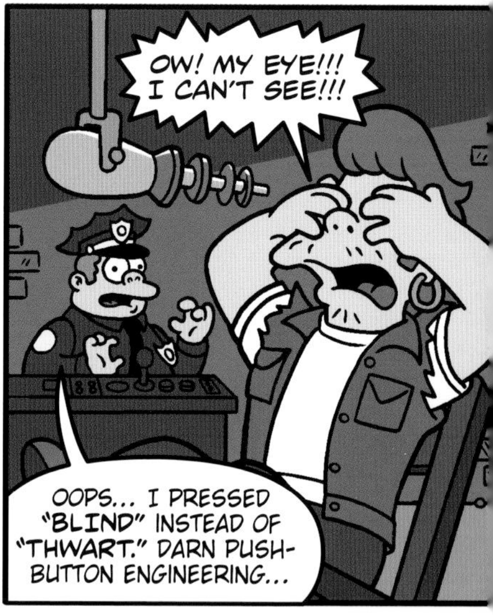
OW! MY EYE!!! I CAN'T SEE!!!
OOPS... I PRESSED "BLIND" INSTEAD OF "THWART." DARN PUSH-BUTTON ENGINEERING...

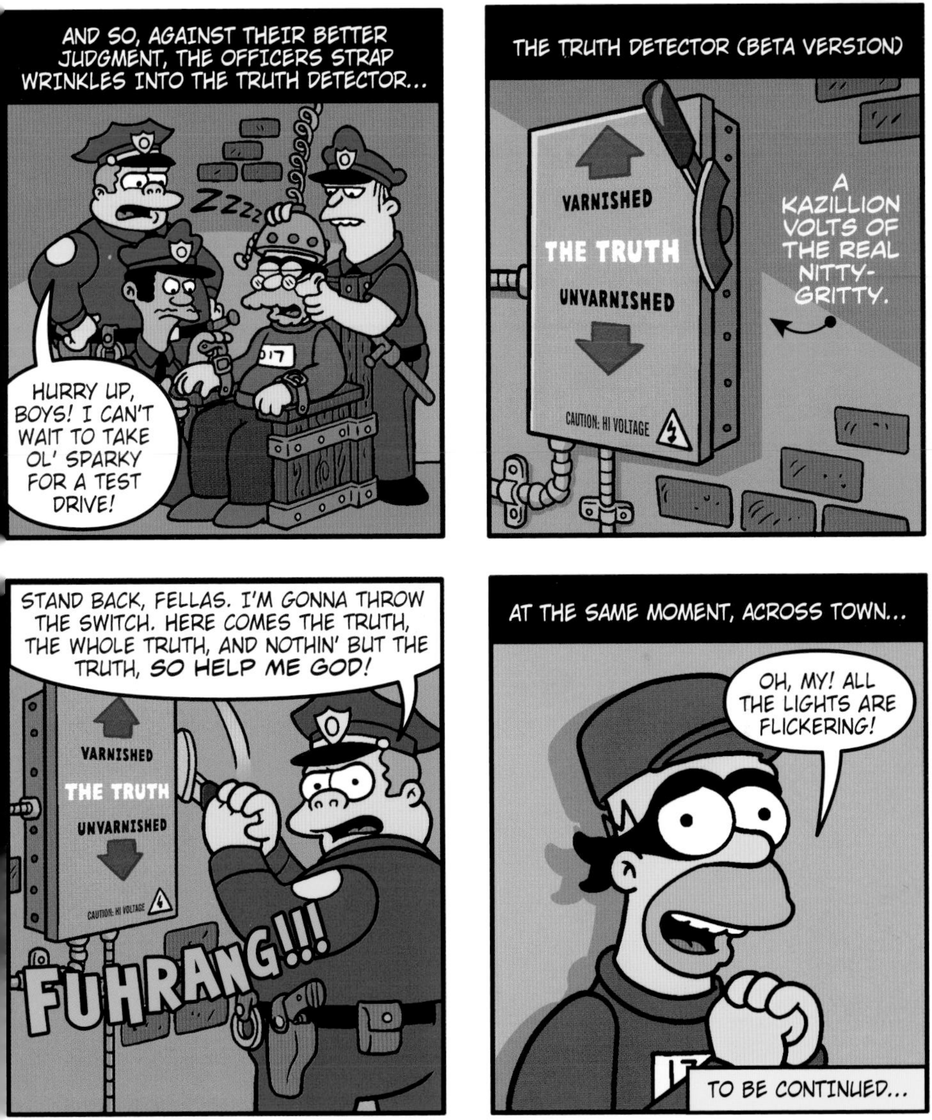

AND SO, AGAINST THEIR BETTER JUDGMENT, THE OFFICERS STRAP WRINKLES INTO THE TRUTH DETECTOR...
ZZZZ
017
HURRY UP, BOYS! I CAN'T WAIT TO TAKE OL' SPARKY FOR A TEST DRIVE!
THE TRUTH DETECTOR (BETA VERSION)
VARNISHED
THE TRUTH
UNVARNISHED
CAUTION: HI VOLTAGE
A KAZILLION VOLTS OF THE REAL NITTY-GRITTY.
STAND BACK, FELLAS. I'M GONNA THROW THE SWITCH. HERE COMES THE TRUTH, THE WHOLE TRUTH, AND NOTHIN' BUT THE TRUTH, SO HELP ME GOD!
VARNISHED
THE TRUTH
UNVARNISHED
CAUTION: HI VOLTAGE
FUHRANG!!!
AT THE SAME MOMENT, ACROSS TOWN...
OH, MY! ALL THE LIGHTS ARE FLICKERING!
TO BE CONTINUED...

THE SPRINGFIELD MAFIA

FAT TONY AND KNOWN ASSOCIATES

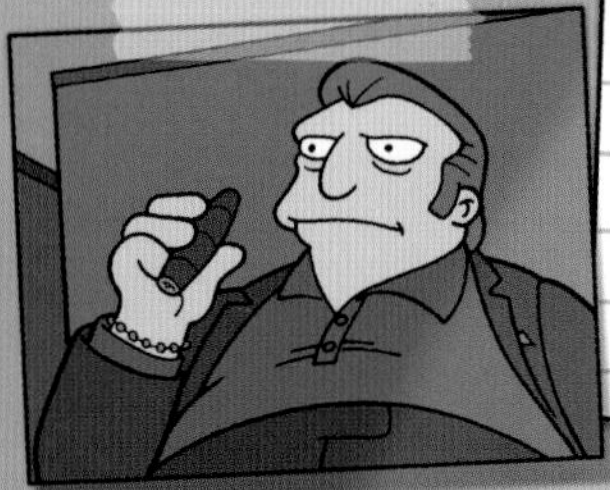

Capo: ANTHONY "FAT TONY" D'AMICO; aliases: William Williams, Marion, Whattayu Lookin' At? Affiliations: Legitimate Businessman's Social Club, Our Waste Management Thing, Springfield Republican Club, Rat Milk Bootleggers Local 929.

NO PHOTO AVAILABLE

MRS. FAT TONY
Whacked by natural causes

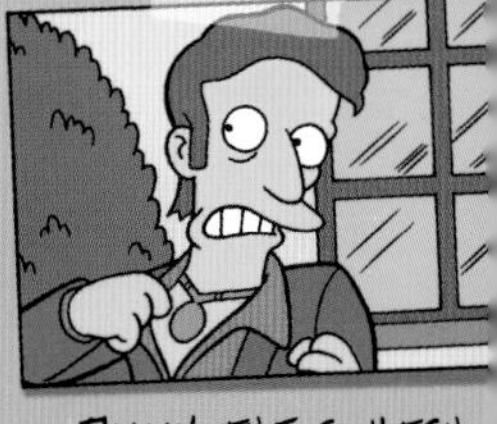

JIMMY THE SNITCH
Possible snitch.

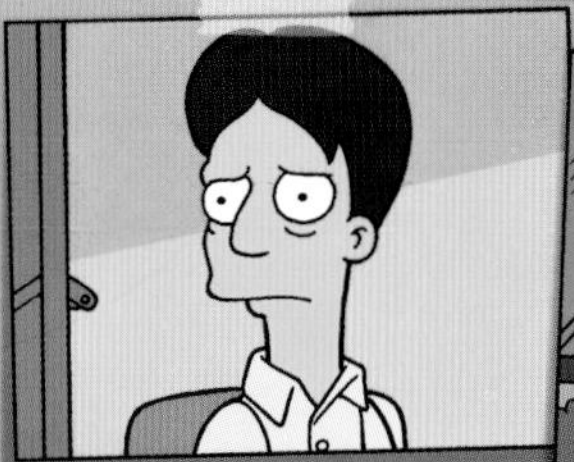

MICHAEL D'AMICO, son
Wants to be a cook.
Makes a decent soufflé.

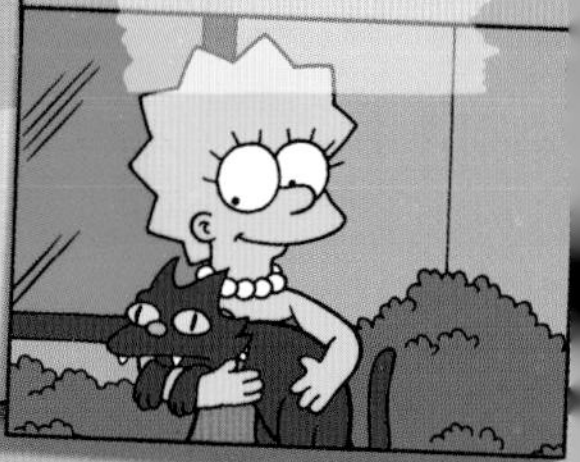

LISA SIMPSON
Possible romantic link to Michael D'Amico.

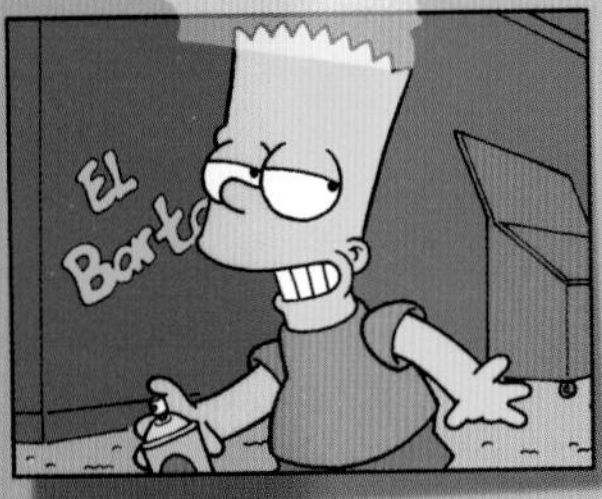
El
Bart

BART SIMPSON
onetime bartender and gofer à la "Goodfellas."

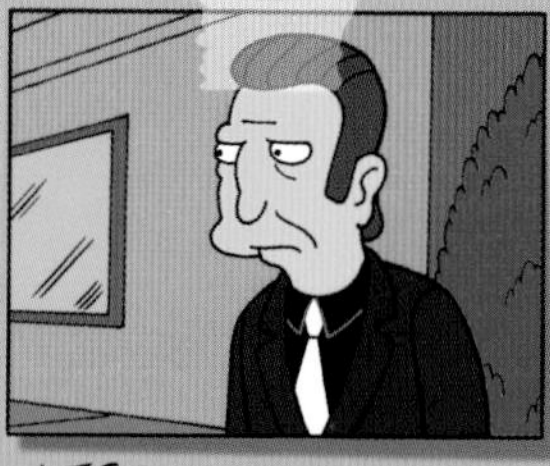

LEGS NOLASTNAME
Gangster/criminal/suspicious type.

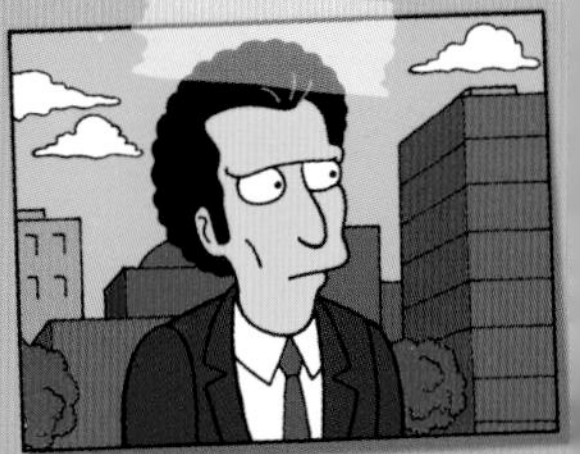

LOUIE LOUIE
Oh no. Said we gotta go.

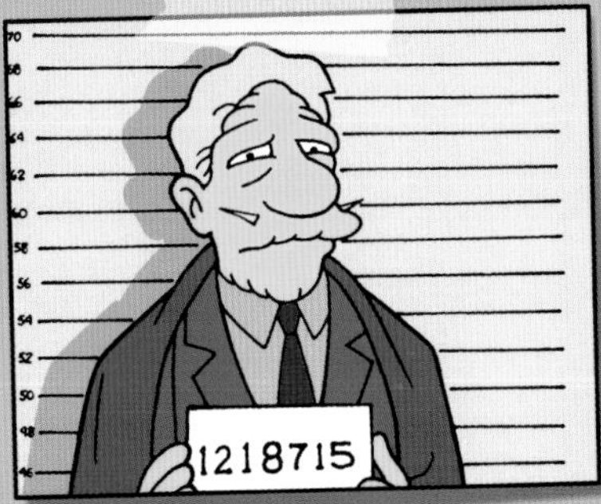
1218715

Capo di Tutti Capo: DON VITTORIO DIMAGGIO
Not actually named "Don."

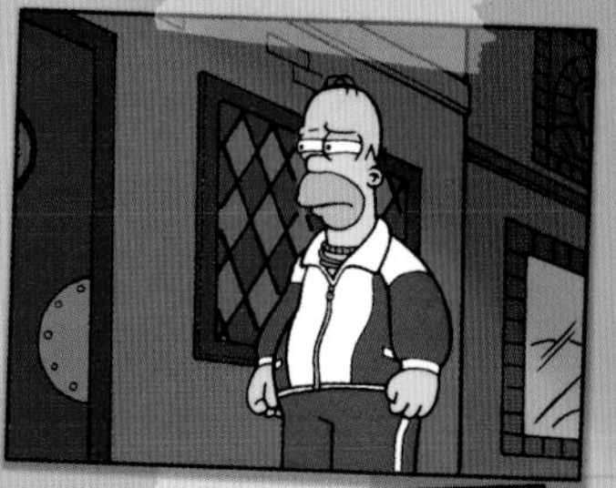

HOMER SIMPSON
Part-time wise guy. Not very wise.

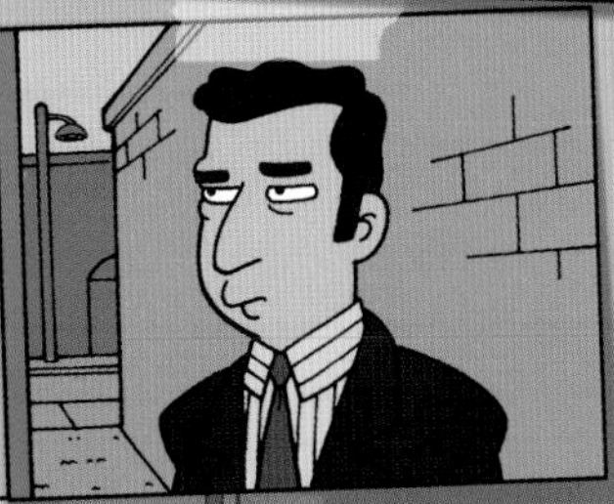

JOHNNY TIGHTLIPS
No comment.

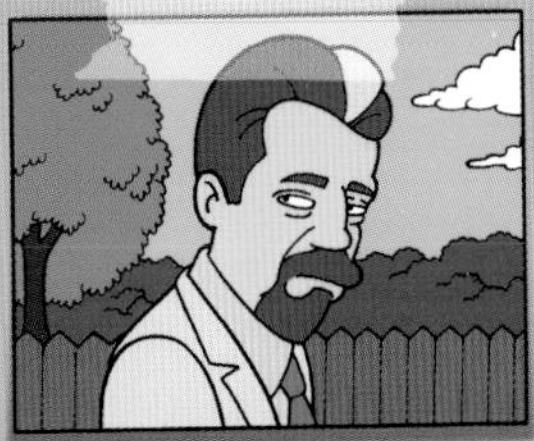

JOE MANTEGNA
Actor. Played Fat Tony in TV movie "Blood on the Blackboard."

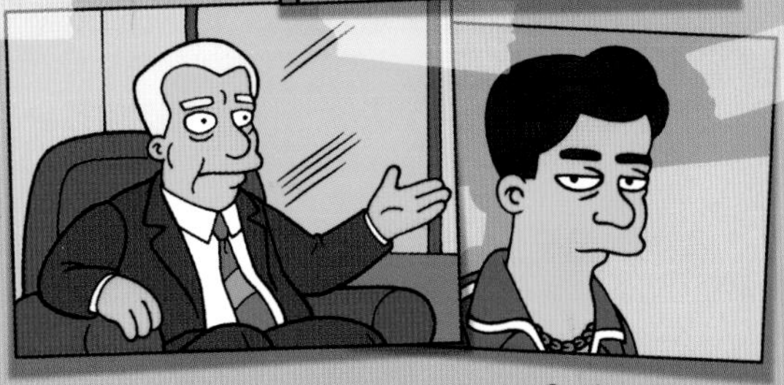

Rivals: DANTE CALABRESE SR. & JR.
Throwaway characters.

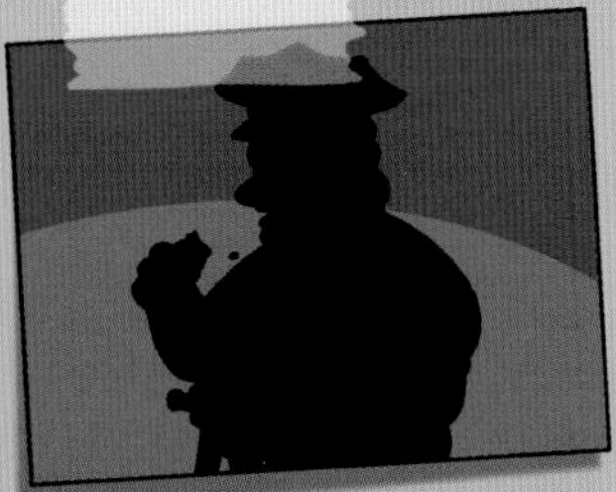

UNKNOWN BAGMAN
Possible $$$ link to Mayor Quimby.

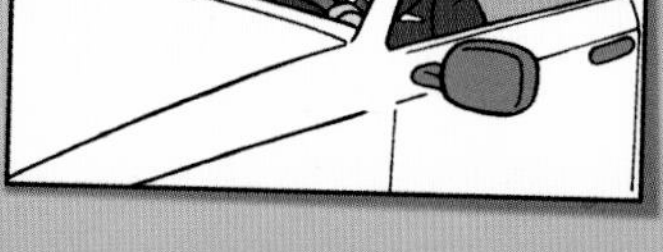

CASTELLANETA FAMILY
Not our problem.

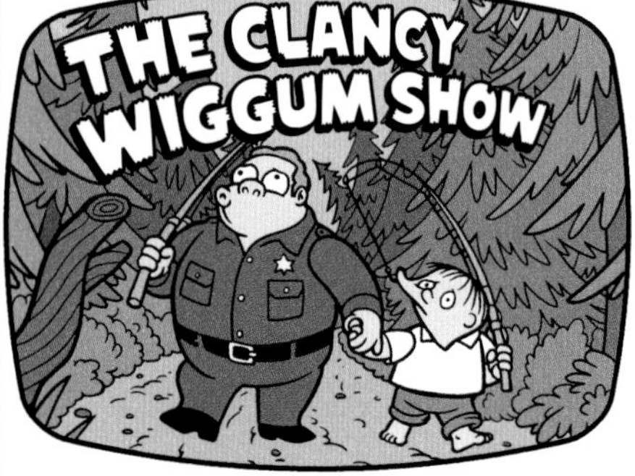
THE CLANCY WIGGUM SHOW

Announcer: "The Clancy Wiggum Show" is brought to you by Pablum Cereal. Another fine product from Generic Foods!

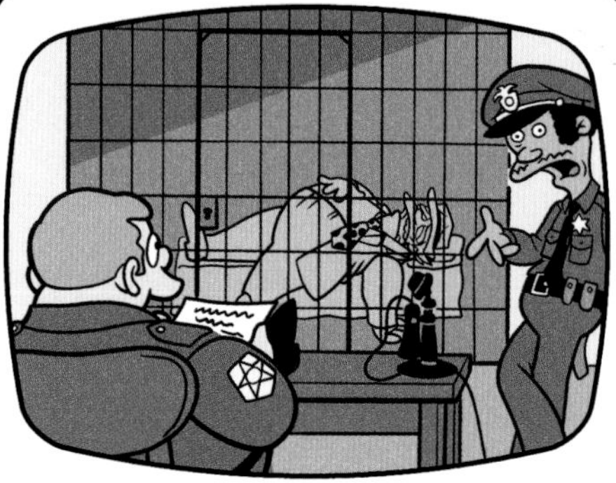

Sheriff Wiggum: Says here the Springfield Gun Nuts Club is having its moonlight duck hunt this evening.
Deputy Lou: Tonight? But I promised Charquelle I'd take her to the church dance!

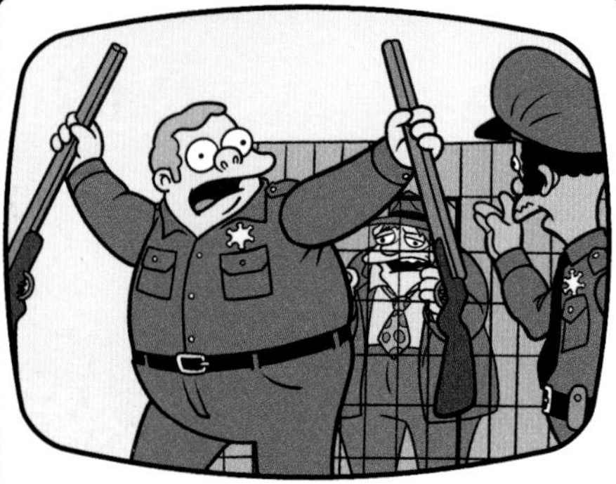

Wiggum: Better order your priorities. Moonlight duck hunts only happen every coupla days.
Barney: If it was up to me, I'd rather go to the hunt than sit in this stinking cell.
Lou: Well, luckily it's not up to you, rummy.

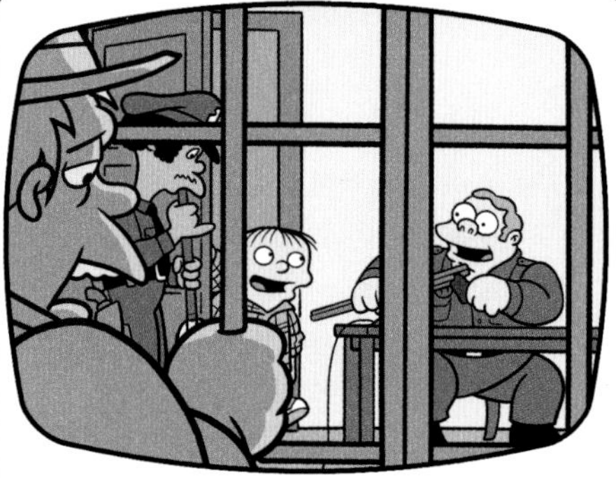

Barney: But I'm the Gun Nuts Club president.
Ralph: Hi, Pa. Hi, Deputy Lou. Hi, Drinking Man.
Wiggum: Oh, Ralphie, you're just in time to help me clean my gun for the big shoot-off Officer Lou and I will be attending tonight. (The phone rings.)

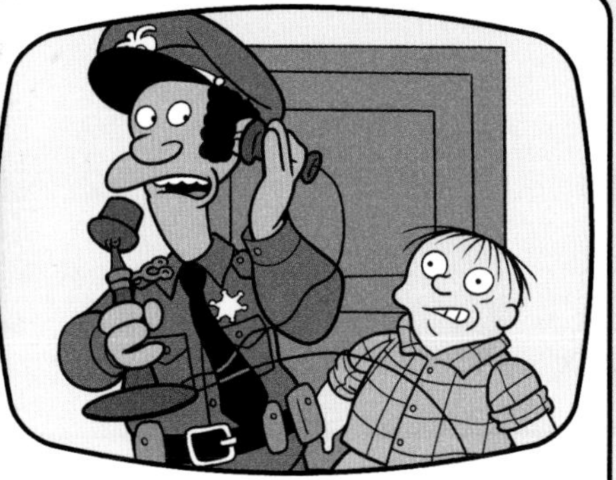

Lou: Sheriff's office. Oh hi, Charquelle. Look, something's come up at the jail. I can't make our date tonight. Yes, something important. What's that? You can't make it either? How come?

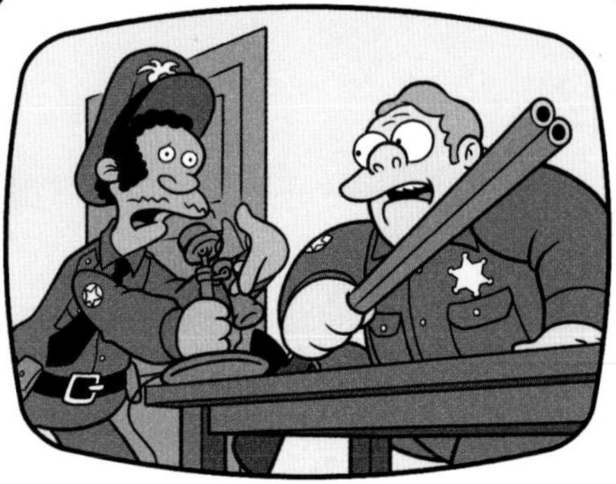

Lou: Charquelle said she and the other tellers at the bank are being held hostage in a robbery.

Wiggum: Holy smokes! We better get down there. Ralphie, keep an eye on things while we're gone.

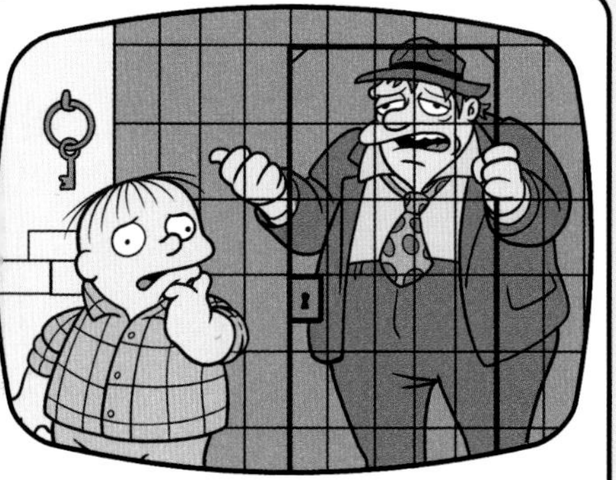

Ralph: Deputy Lou lied to the telephone lady.

Barney: He sure did. But you know what will make things better? If you hand me those keys over there.

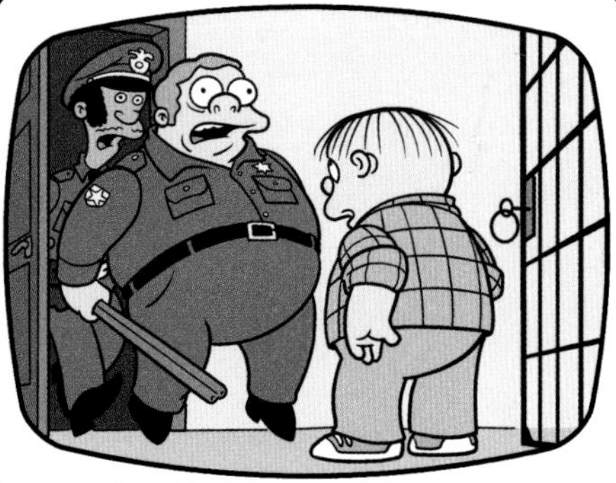

Lou: Too bad the robbers got away. We'll get 'em next time...eh, Sheriff?

Wiggum: What the--?! Where's Barney? Ralphie, did you let Barney out?

Ralph: Uh...no...robbers...with keys...let him out. And that's not a lie.

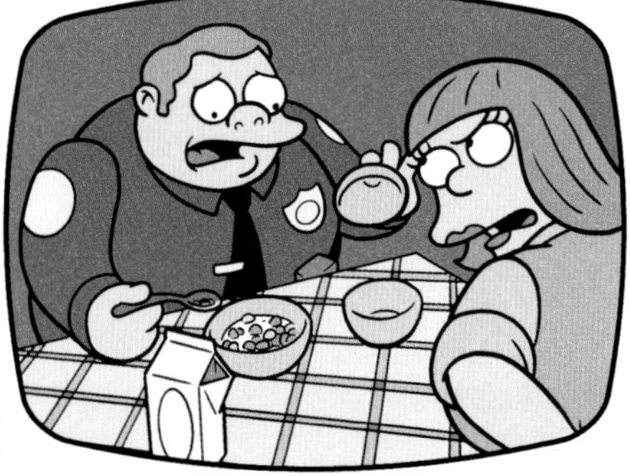

Wiggum: We're out of sugar! Sarah, eating Pablum Cereal without sugar is downright criminal.
Sarah Wiggum: Clancy, if you don't like this cereal, you can strap me to the electric chair!

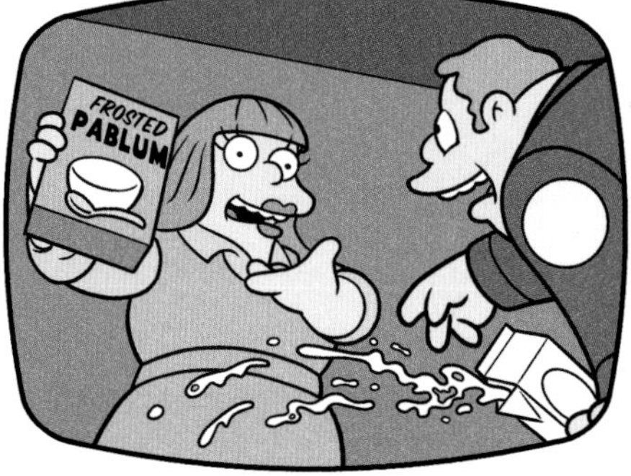
FROSTED PABLUM

Sarah: This is new Sugar-Frosted Pablum Cereal!
Wiggum: Sugar-Frosted Pablum? Case closed!
Jingle Singers: The only way / To start your day / Is to start your day / The Pablum way!

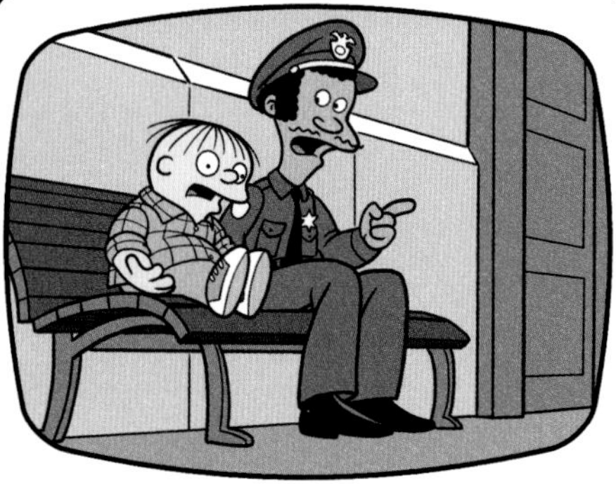

Ralph: It's wrong to tell a lie, isn't it?
Lou: Well, uh, most of the time.

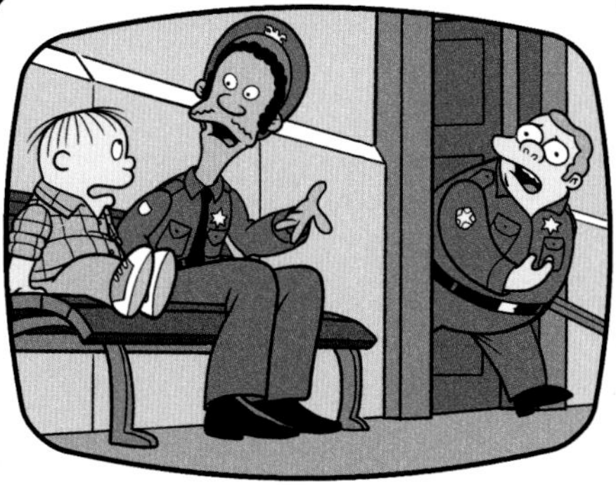

Ralph: I've heard of daytime and nighttime but when is "mostofthe" time?
Lou: Well, uh, you see, kid--
Wiggum: Can the chatter, Deputy. We've got another robbery in progress over at Kwikie's Service Station!

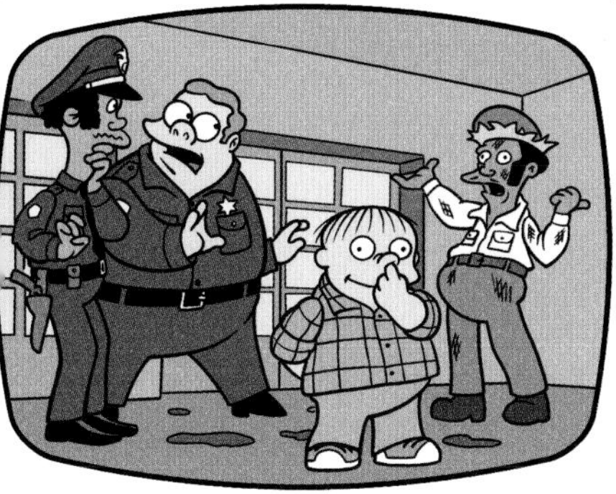

Wiggum: Now, calm down, Apoober. Just tell us what happened.

Apoober: Oh, my stars and bars, it was terrible! A robber made me give him the money in my cash register and then he ran out the back door, y'all!

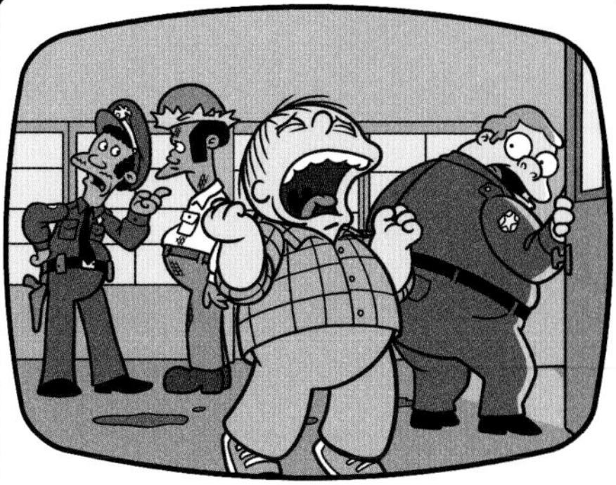

Lou: Is that the truth? You better not be lying. Believe me, it's better to tell the truth than to lie.

Ralph: I admit it! I lied! I let the drinking man out of the cage!

Wiggum: Is that so, Ralphie? Well, that makes you...

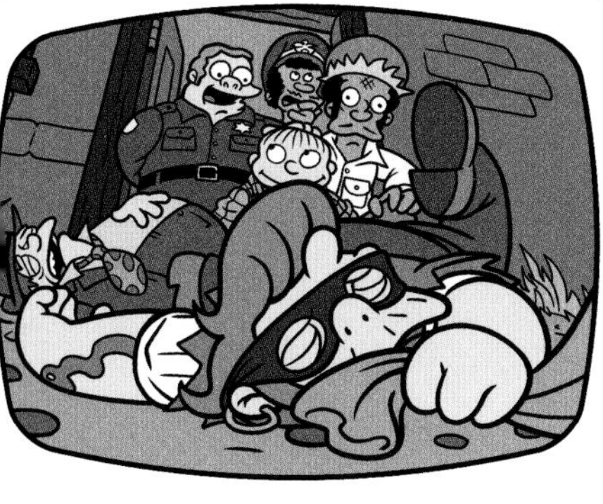

Wiggum: ...a hero! If you hadn't let Barney out, he wouldn't have passed out in this gutter and tripped up the robber.

Lou: Hmmm. Maybe I better start telling the truth, too.

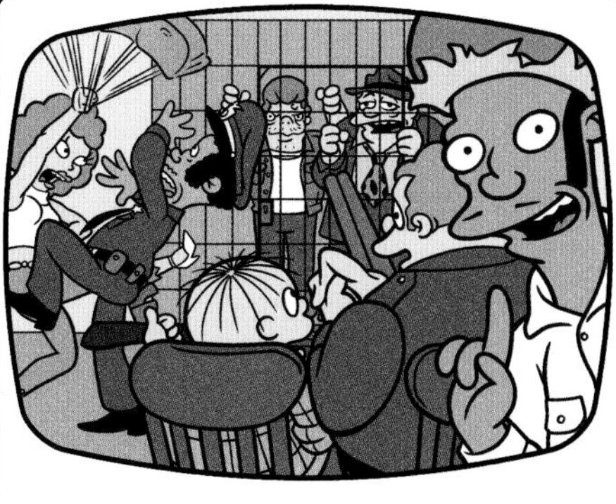

Charquelle: You were going to go hunting instead of taking me to the dance? You liar!

Ralph: This is one time that isn't "mostofthe" time.

Wiggum: Whatever you say, Ralphie.

Apoober: Y'all come again now, ya hear?

ANATOMY OF A POLICE CHIEF

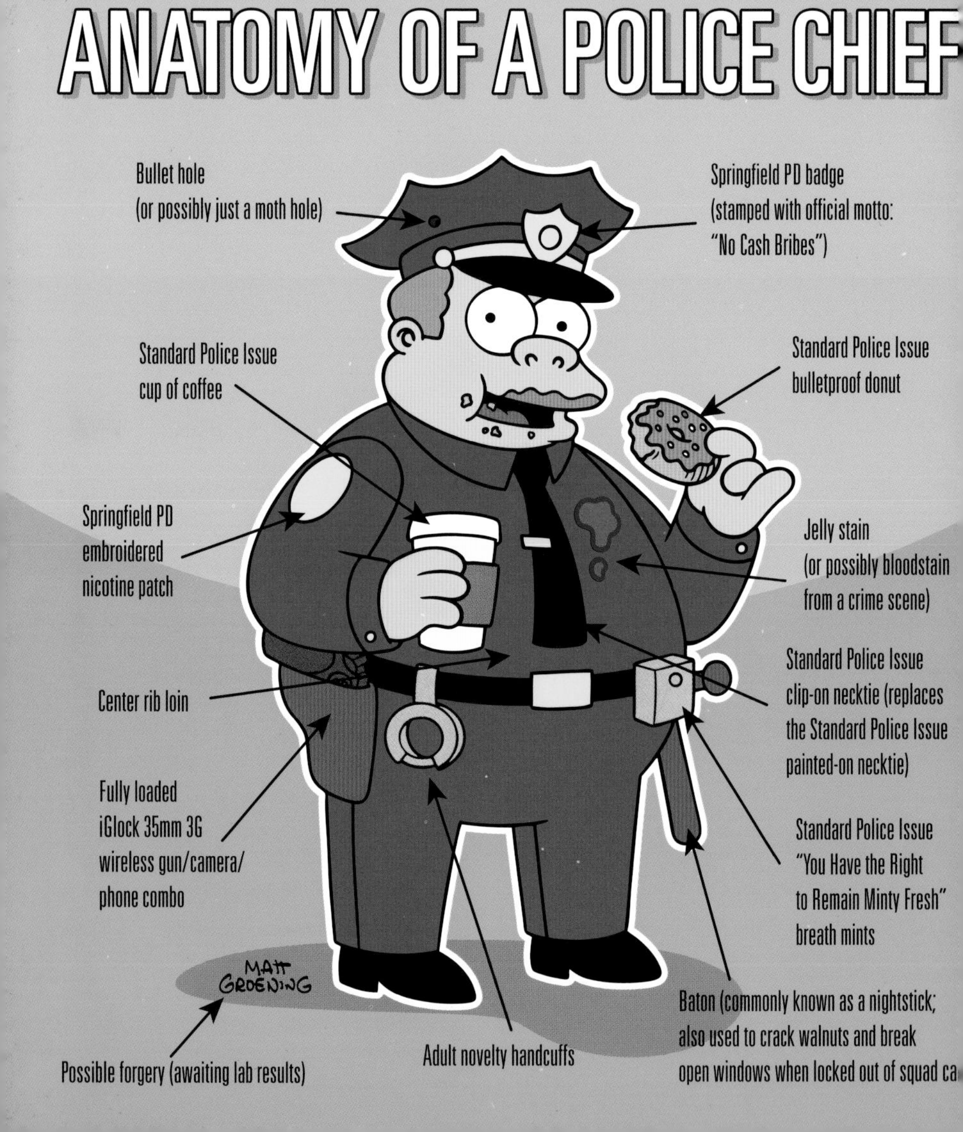
Bullet hole
(or possibly just a moth hole)
Springfield PD badge
(stamped with official motto:
"No Cash Bribes")
Standard Police Issue
cup of coffee
Standard Police Issue
bulletproof donut
Springfield PD
embroidered
nicotine patch
Jelly stain
(or possibly bloodstain
from a crime scene)
Standard Police Issue
clip-on necktie (replaces
the Standard Police Issue
painted-on necktie)
Center rib loin
Fully loaded
iGlock 35mm 3G
wireless gun/camera/
phone combo
Standard Police Issue
"You Have the Right
to Remain Minty Fresh"
breath mints
MATT
GROENING
Baton (commonly known as a nightstick;
also used to crack walnuts and break
open windows when locked out of squad ca
Adult novelty handcuffs
Possible forgery (awaiting lab results)

WHAT'S ON WIGGUM'S MIND?

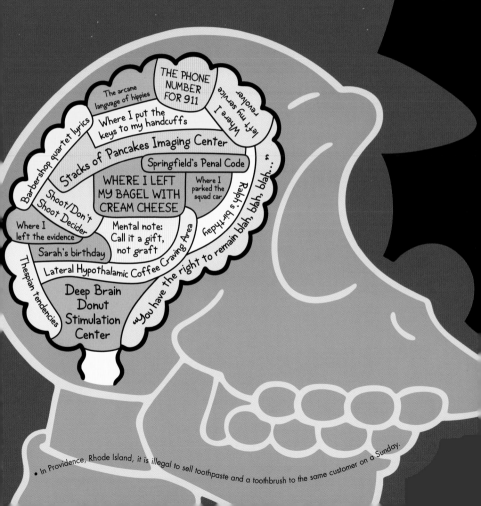

The arcane language of hippies

THE PHONE NUMBER FOR 911

Where I left my service revolver

Barbershop quartet lyrics

Where I put the keys to my handcuffs

Stacks of Pancakes Imaging Center

Springfield's Penal Code

WHERE I LEFT MY BAGEL WITH CREAM CHEESE

Where I parked the squad car

Shoot/Don't Shoot Decider

Where I left the evidence

Mental note: Call it a gift, not graft

"Ralph's birthday"

Sarah's birthday

Lateral Hypothalamic Coffee Craving Area

"You have the right to remain blah, blah, blah..."

Thespian tendencies

Deep Brain Donut Stimulation Center

• In Providence, Rhode Island, it is illegal to sell toothpaste and a toothbrush to the same customer on a Sunday.

WIGGUM SINGS 'EM

THE SNACK BREAK SONG

(sung to the tune of "She'll Be Comin' 'Round the Mountain")

I am eating chocolate pudding
with my thumbs!
I am eating chocolate pudding
with my thumbs!
I am sitting at my desk,
I am sitting at my desk,
I am eating chocolate pudding
with my thumbs!

• It is illegal to flag down a taxi in London if you have the plague.

THE DRIVE-THRU SONG

(sung to the tune of "London Bridge")

I buy burgers from a clown,
From a clown, from a clown!
I buy burgers from a clown
And fried cupcakes! (They're new!)

THE BUST-IN SONG

(sung to the tune of "Farmer in the Dell")

I like kicking in doors!
I like kicking in doors!
I hope they don't have a deadbolt
'Cause I like kicking in doors!

THE BUYING DONUTS AT THE LARD LAD SONG

(sung to the tune of "Auld Lang Syne")

These dozen donuts that I bought
Are mine, mine, all mine!
I will feel a deep sense of shame
When I get back in line!

THE RIOT SONG

(sung to the tune of "Buffalo Gals")

Drunken sports fans, I'm watchin' 'em fight,
Watchin' 'em fight, watchin' 'em fight...
Drunken sports fans, I'm watchin' 'em fight...
And singing about it in this tune!

THE LOADING THE CRIMINAL INTO THE CRUISER SONG

(sung to the tune of "Twinkle, Twinkle, Little Star")

Pipe down, scumbag, get in back,
Or I will give you a whack.
You should not have stolen that car,
Wait for me while I'm in the bar.
Pipe down, scumbag, if you stay here,
I will bring you back a beer.

THE PARKING SONG

(sung to the tune of "Joy to the World")

I can park!
Wherever I want!
It rules! It rules! It rules!
In front of someone's driveway!
No one can ever say,
"You can't park that car there!
I'll kick your derrière!"
Because I am the chief
I park without a care!

YELLOW

(sung to the tune of Coldplay's "Yellow")

I'm sorry, sir,
But I don't believe you
When you say it's true
That the light was yellow.
I think it was red
And that you still went through,
Got a broken taillight, too.
You're one unlucky fellow.

SINCE U SHOPLIFTED NEXT TO CHEF WONG'S

(sung to the tune of Kelly Clarkson's "Since U Been Gone")

I like Chef Wong's!
Moo goo gai pan and
some plum wine!
Eatin' wontons, yeah, yeah...
Thanks to you, next door,
shoplifting sarongs...
I'm at Chef Wong's!

• Monkeys are forbidden to smoke cigarettes in South Bend, Indiana.

THE CLOTHES SHOPPING SONG

(sung to the tune of the Ramones' "I Wanna Be Sedated")

Twenty, twenty, twenty percent off I'll pay!
It's the standard cop discount!
If you want 911 to work after today,
Give me the standard cop discount!
Get me some new slacks!
Some really stylish boots!
Mercy, mercy, mercy!
That outfit's just too cute!
Is that a guy robbing the store?
Here's my gun, please don't shoot!
Oh no, oh no, oh no!

THE DANGEROUS DRIVING SONG

(sung to the tune of "Hark, the Herald Angels Sing")

Cars are fun to jump over things!
While I'm eating hot, hot wings!
Blue cheese dressing very nice
"OH MY GOD A SCHOOL BUS!"

CLANCY WIGGUM

MAN OF CLANDESTINY

THE MANY UNDERCOVER DISGUISES OF CHIEF WIGGUM

Horatio L. Gigglebottom,
English Fishmonger

Despair Incarnate,
Disaffected Goth Youth

• In Illinois, the officially recognized language is not "English" but "American."

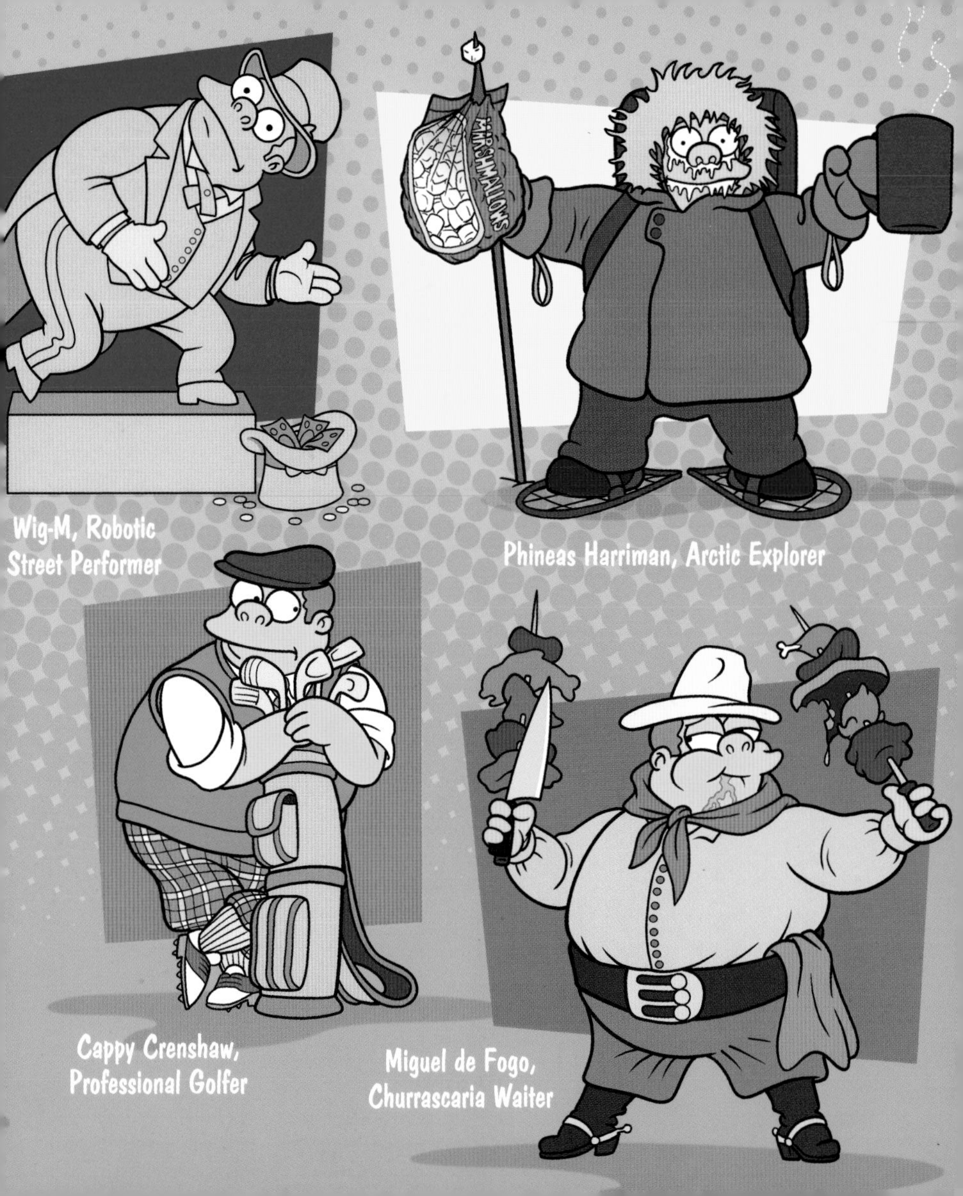

MARSHMALLOWS

Wig-M, Robotic Street Performer

Phineas Harriman, Arctic Explorer

Cappy Crenshaw, Professional Golfer

Miguel de Fogo, Churrascaria Waiter

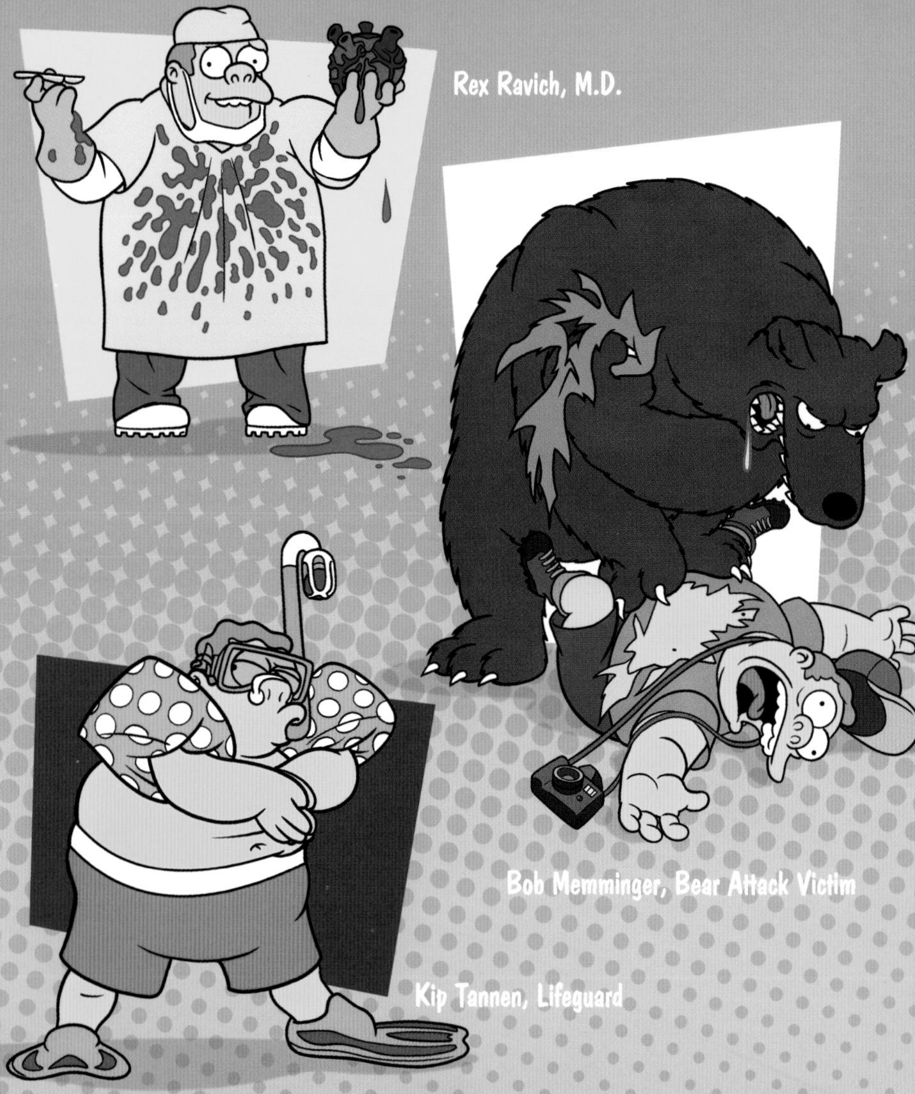
Rex Ravich, M.D.
Bob Memminger, Bear Attack Victim
Kip Tannen, Lifeguard

• In Saco, Missouri, women are forbidden from wearing hats that might frighten timid persons, children, or animals.

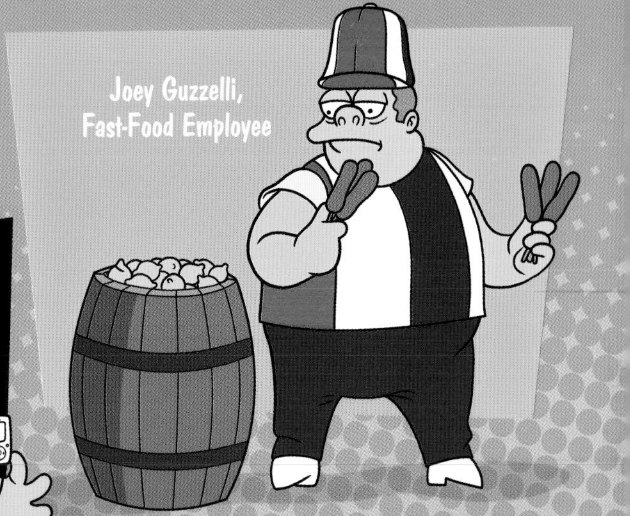
Joey Guzzelli,
Fast-Food Employee

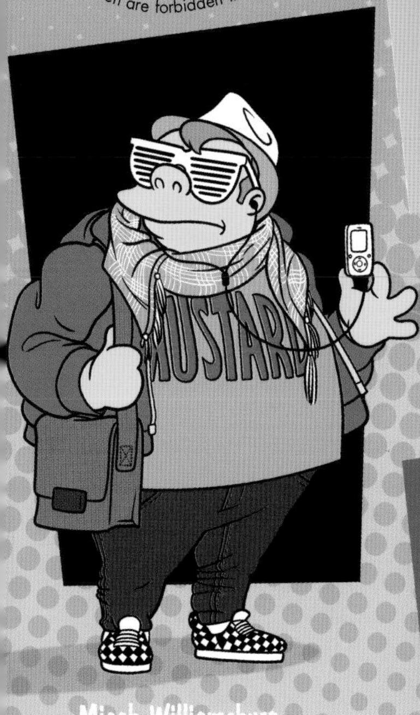
MUSTARD
Micah Williamsburg,
Utterly "Over It" Hipster

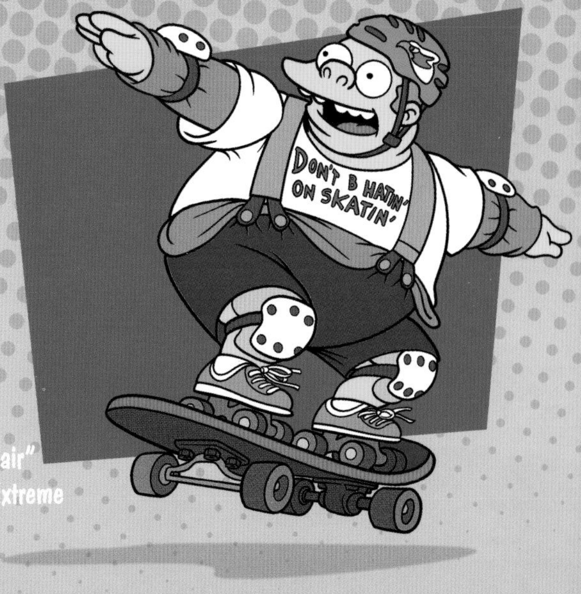
DON'T B HATIN' ON SKATIN'
Slam "Gravelhair"
McBodyheimer, Extreme
Athlete

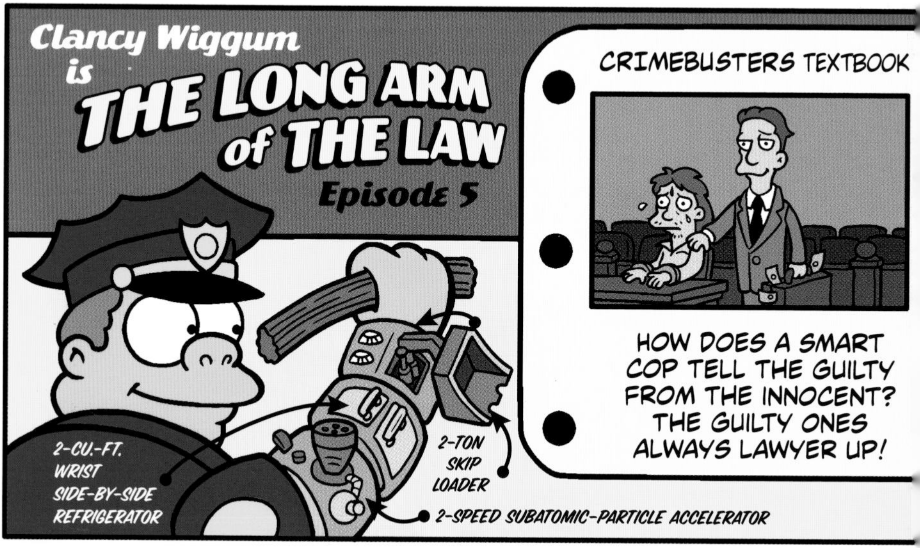
Clancy Wiggum
is
THE LONG ARM of THE LAW
Episode 5
CRIMEBUSTERS TEXTBOOK
HOW DOES A SMART COP TELL THE GUILTY FROM THE INNOCENT? THE GUILTY ONES ALWAYS LAWYER UP!
2-CU.-FT. WRIST SIDE-BY-SIDE REFRIGERATOR
2-TON SKIP LOADER
2-SPEED SUBATOMIC-PARTICLE ACCELERATOR

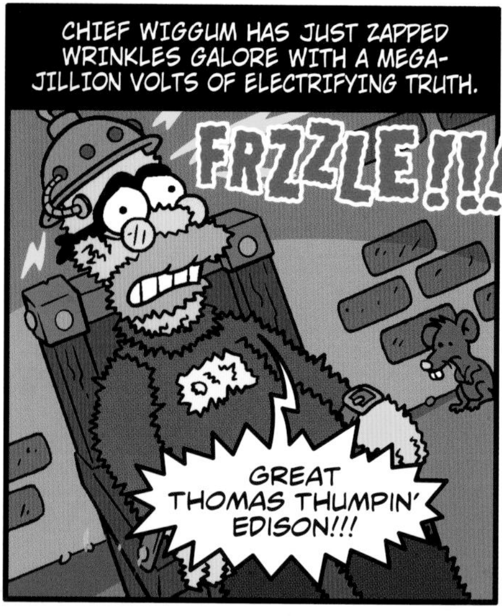
CHIEF WIGGUM HAS JUST ZAPPED WRINKLES GALORE WITH A MEGA-JILLION VOLTS OF ELECTRIFYING TRUTH.
FRZZLE!!!
GREAT THOMAS THUMPIN' EDISON!!!

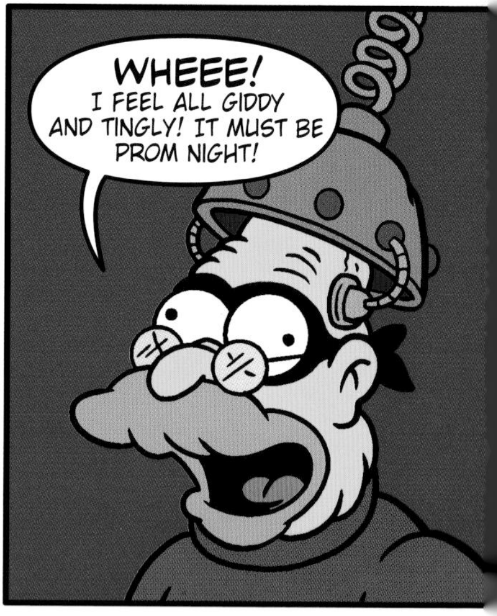
WHEEE! I FEEL ALL GIDDY AND TINGLY! IT MUST BE PROM NIGHT!

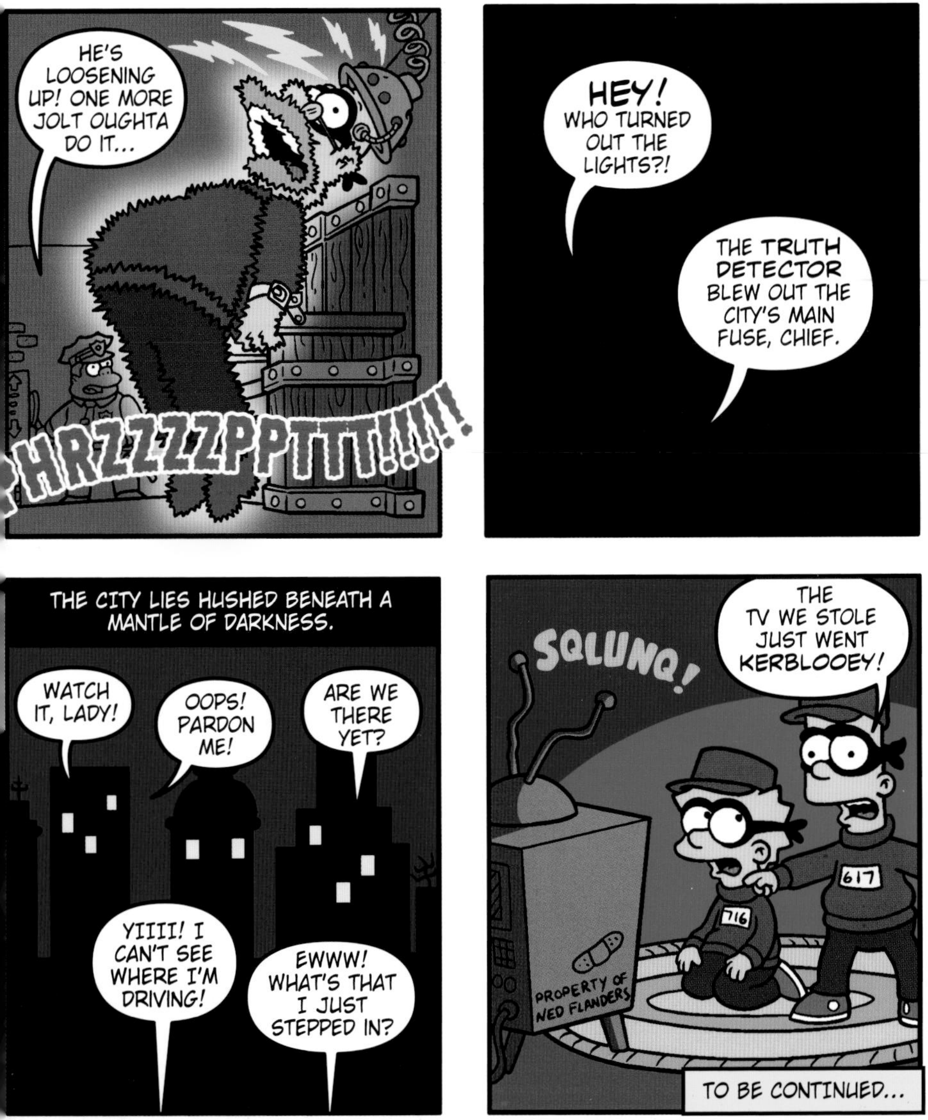
HE'S LOOSENING UP! ONE MORE JOLT OUGHTA DO IT...
HRZZZZZPPTTTT!!!!!
HEY! WHO TURNED OUT THE LIGHTS?!
THE TRUTH DETECTOR BLEW OUT THE CITY'S MAIN FUSE, CHIEF.
THE CITY LIES HUSHED BENEATH A MANTLE OF DARKNESS.
WATCH IT, LADY!
OOPS! PARDON ME!
ARE WE THERE YET?
YIIII! I CAN'T SEE WHERE I'M DRIVING!
EWWW! WHAT'S THAT I JUST STEPPED IN?
SQLUNQ!
THE TV WE STOLE JUST WENT KERBLOOEY!
PROPERTY OF NED FLANDERS
716
617
TO BE CONTINUED...

THE MOST IMPORTANT MEAL OF THE DAY JUST GOT IMPORTANTER!

The Springfield Police Department Pancake Breakfast!

(a benefit to raise money for a really cool police officers' lounge we want to build in one of the cells)

This Saturday 8:00 – 10:00 A.M.!

Featuring:

- 100% Arabica Police Brew-tality! •
- Eddie's "I Smell Bacon" and Eggs! •
- French-Toasted Jelly Donuts! •
- Wiggum's "So Awfully Good They're Unlawful" Waffles! •
- Extreme Maple Syrup (with bits o' bark)! •
- Lou's Deviled Eggs Benedict (the secret is the pepper spray!) •
- Tasered Taters! •
- A Selection of Warmed Breads Recovered from Recent Drug Arrests! •

Breakfast served in the department's holding cell!
Free breathalyzer tests!
One lucky breakfaster will win a five-minute shopping spree in the SPD's Evidence Locker!
Music by Ralph Wiggum and the Paste-Eaters!

Whether you're hungry for justice or thirsty for juice, be there this Saturday!

Wiggum vs. McGriff the Crime Dog

McGriff the Crime Dog	Wiggum the Crime Human
"TAKE A BITE OUT OF CRIME"	"TAKE A BITE OUT OF CRULLER"
PUG NOSE	PIG NOSE
INSISTENT BARK	INCESSANT BABBLE
SOUNDS LIKE ROBERT STACK	SOUNDS LIKE EDWARD G. ROBINSON
PADDED PAWS	PADDED BELLY
REGULARLY SEEN ON TV COMMERCIALS	REGULARLY WATCHES TV COMMERCIALS
PROTECTIVE OVERCOAT	PRONOUNCED OVERBITE
INSTINCTS LIKE A BLOODHOUND	STINKS LIKE A BASSET HOUND
WAS HEAD OF THE CLASS AT POLICE ACADEMY	SAW "HEAD OF THE CLASS" AND "POLICE ACADEMY"
FOUR FEET	FLAT FEET
ETHICAL, MORAL, AND CONSCIENTIOUS	ENJOYS CHOCOLATE

• It is against the law to read a comic book while operating a motor vehicle in Oklahoma.

THE FOLLOWING ARE FOUR PAGES FROM THE FINAL EPISODE OF "WIGGUM, P.I.," THE SHORT-LIVED SPIN-OFF SERIES STARRING CHIEF WIGGUM. THE HANDWRITTEN COMMENTS ARE FROM AN EXECUTIVE WITH THE OOEEDATGOOD CAJUN SPICE AND VOODOO COMPANY, SPONSORS OF THE SHOW

WIGGUM, P.I.

"The Big Queasy"

EXT. NEW ORLEANS FRENCH QUARTER CAFÉ - DAY

DETECTIVE CLANCY WIGGUM sits in a white wicker chair enjoying a bowl of jambalaya.

CHIEF WIGGUM
Nothin' like a big bowl of jambalaya on a hot summer day in New Orleans.

Chief says to make sure there are shakers of Ooeedatgood < Salt and Pepper on the table.

Wiggum lifts a heaping spoonful of gumbo to his lips. Before he can taste it, SEYMOUR SKINNER (A.K.A. "Skinny Boy") runs up and interrupts.

SKINNY BOY
Chief Wiggum, I got some bad news for you.

CHIEF WIGGUM
Can't it wait until I'm finished eating?

Suggested rewrite: "Can't it wait until I've finished eating my jambalaya made with Ooeedatgood Jambalaya Seasoning. Ooeedatgood!"

SKINNY BOY
It can't wait all day, no. The fate of N'Orleans is on the line.

CHIEF WIGGUM
Say, why do you say "N'Orleans"?

SKINNY BOY
It's just my native accent. Just like native N'Yorkers used to call their home N'Amsterdam. But there's no time for dialect analysis. Big Daddy's back in town!

Chief Wiggum drops his spoon.

Can Skinny Boy be wearing an Ooeedatgood Cajun Spice hat?

CHIEF WIGGUM
Big Daddy! That ol' smuggler. What's he up to this time?

• In Washington, it is an offense to pretend that you have rich parents.

SKINNY BOY

Smugglin'! I got a hot tip from our
favorite snitch, Huggy Bug.

Can he say "spicy" instead?

Chief Wiggum gets up.

CHIEF WIGGUM

Well, c'mon, that tip won't stay hot
forever. (OFF-SCREEN RE: THE
JAMBALAYA) Can I get this to go?

INT. CAJUN RESTAURANT - SOON AFTER

HUGGY BUG is a cool dude in a big white hat, white jacket, and black
shirt unbuttoned down to the belt. Chief Wiggum and Skinny Boy are
sitting on either side of him in a booth. He has a plate of shrimp
Creole in front of him.

Can he be wearing an Ooeedatgood Cajun Spice shirt? And hat, too?

HUGGY BUG

Looky hyere, I doe-no nuthin'.

SKINNY BOY

Lighten up, Huggy. It's me, Skinny
Boy. You can tell me what you told me
before.

HUGGY BUG

Not wif him 'round I doen. He not the
cops, and he not my mama. I doe-no
nuthin'.

ADD: "My mama cooks with Ooeedatgood Cajun Spices and Voodoo Herbs!"

CHIEF WIGGUM

You better start talking to me or
you'll wish I was your mama. What's
all this about Big Daddy being back in
the crawfish smuggling business?

HUGGY BUG

Look, you dinnuh hyear nuthin' from
me…

SKINNY BOY

No, not so far…

HUGGY BUG

…but you head on down 'bout the
warehouse district 'round midnight,
an' you see where yat.

Can it be the "spice district" instead? Or the "Voodoo district"?

A WAITRESS puts a plate in front of Wiggum and another in front of Skinner.

> WAITRESS
> Po'boy sandwich with red beans and rice for you and muffuletas and andouille sausage gumbo for you.

Rewrite:
"Did you know that Ooeedatgood makes red beans and rice seasoning and muffuleta pepper? Also Zombie Guard Brand® Garlic."

> CHIEF WIGGUM
> Oh boy! Let's dig in!

> SKINNY BOY
> Warehouse district 'round midnight, eh? It's almost 11:30 now. We better get these orders to go. 'Cause that's what we have--to go!

INT. WAREHOUSE - LATER

Chief Wiggum (holding two white takeout bags) and Skinny Boy (holding one bag and a lidded Styrofoam cup) slowly turn the corner around a large stack of shipping crates.

> CHIEF WIGGUM
> It's quiet. Too quiet. You think we missed the drop?

> SKINNY BOY
> Maybe. I told you we shouldn't have stopped for those pralines and sweet potato pie.

...made with Ooeedatgood Praline Pecan Chunks.

> CHIEF WIGGUM
> Yeah, well what took so long was your order!

> SKINNY BOY
> Can I help it if I need a café au lait with my beignet?

We don't make beignet ingredients.

> CHIEF WIGGUM
> *Can it be a voodoo doll instead?* No, I guess not. Hey, wait a minute, maybe we're not too late at all. Take a look at this!

Chief Wiggum points to a crate that's marked "Big Daddy's Crawfish." The word "crawfish" is peeling off. Chief Wiggum tears it off and underneath it says "Turduckens."

SKINNY BOY
Do you think Big Daddy is using these crates to smuggle crawfish disguised as turduckens?

Maybe he could be smuggling spices or Voodoo gris-gris bags?

CHIEF WIGGUM
No, I think he's using these crates to smuggle turduckens disguised as crawfish!

A shadowy figure (BIG DADDY) sneaks up behind them.

BIG DADDY
You're both wrong! I'm using these crates to smuggle crates!

Big Daddy hits each of the men over the back of their heads with a blackjack in each hand. They fall limply to the ground.

INT. WAREHOUSE - LATER

Chief Wiggum and Skinny Boy are tied together and are hanging from a hook on the end of a crane that dangles precariously over a vat of boiling oil. Big Daddy laughs as they come to.

BIG DADDY
Wake up, sleepyheads! Bath time.

How about, "It's Ooeedatgood time!"

CHIEF WIGGUM
Big Daddy! You fiend!! What have you done with our takeout orders?

BIG DADDY
All in good time, Fatman and RobSkin.

CHIEF WIGGUM
You should talk. You weigh more than I do.

BIG DADDY
Muscle weighs more than fat. I was strong enough to haul your butts up over that vat, wasn't I?

CHIEF WIGGUM
The only thing strong about you is... your smell!

Add "Almost as strong as the smell of Ooeedatgood Voodoo Incense" or "That better be a cauldron of Ooeedatgood Cajun Cookin' Oil. We want our boiled zombie bodies to taste good!"

DRAMATIC MUSIC STING. END OF SCENE.

• It is illegal to wear a goatee without a license in Massachusetts.

Guns and Buttercups

My Life as a Policewoman

(Reprinted with permission from *Ladies' Home Crime Journal*)

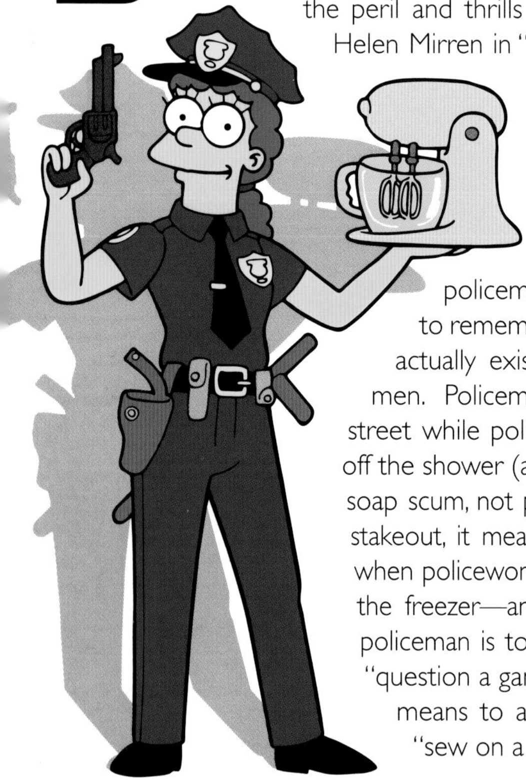

Being a lady cop doesn't always have the danger and excitement of Glenn Close in "Damages" or Helen Mirren in "Prime Suspect." Sometimes it's the peril and thrills of Kyra Sedgwick in "The Closer" or Helen Mirren in "Prime Suspect 2." Other times it's not like a TV show at all, and that means it's a lot like Frances McDormand in *Fargo*.

When you become a cop, something you always have to remember is that policewomen are no different from policemen. What makes that especially difficult to remember are the many, many differences that actually exist between policewomen and policemen. Policemen are told to clean the scum off the street while policewomen are told to clean the scum off the shower (and sometimes the street but only if it's soap scum, not people scum). When policemen take a stakeout, it means watching someone for a long time; when policewomen do it, it means removing meat from the freezer—and broiling it for the squad room! If a policeman is told to "needle a button man" it means "question a gangster." You can probably guess what it means to a policewoman! (If you can't, it means "sew on a button, man.")

As if the metaphorical differences aren't enough, think of the equipment. Every piece of a lady cop's uniform, including the pants, shoes, shirt, hat, and jock strap, is very ill-fitting and uncomfortable—not to mention a fashion nightmare. The billy club, handcuffs, Taser, and other regulation equipment just don't fit easily into a handbag (maybe a diaper bag, but that presents its own problems). Plus, getting used to handling a gun can be extremely intimidating for the uninitiated. Still, after clicking off fifteen rounds on a .40-caliber semiautomatic, double-barreled, melonite Smith & Wesson revolver with stainless-steel, two-toned handle, Zytel polymer frame, and tritium sights, you begin to get used to it.

There are unique challenges for a policewoman in my hometown, Springfield. Outside of the police force itself, there isn't much actual crime in Springfield (we only have one confirmed career criminal named Snake, or sometimes Jailbird), so most of our work is neighborhood support and domestic disturbance calls. Interestingly, about 80 percent of those calls come from my house (and the rest are directed to my house), so I guess you could say that for me, "Challenges begin at home."

Another challenge is dealing with the so-called moral and ethical crimes that don't show up in our statistics (because we don't report them). Speaking of reporting statistics, one of my proudest achievements as a policewoman is convincing my department to create a new statistical category called "Crimes Against Women." They had previously been categorized under "Victimless Crimes."

Probably the biggest challenge of all involves respect when it comes to the police department in particular and the community in general. As a Springfield police-woman, it is very hard to get any and even harder to have any. I can't tell you all the names you get called, but I'll tell you a lot of them (in alphabetical order): Copchick, Copperella, Copperina, Frances Coppola, Honeybadge, Lucy Lawlady, Peggy Piggy, Pistol-Packin' Mama, Policebabe, Señorita Copperita, She-bull, She-cop, She-lady, and those are just the ones my husband uses most often.

(Continued on page 48)

ON WIGGUM'S WATCH

REQUIRED VIEWING FOR THE COP ON THE COUCH

COP TV

5PM
SQUEAL OR NO DEAL (60 MIN.)
Contestants plea-bargain for cash prizes and reduced sentences.

ASAP

6PM
SPRINGFIELD'S FUNNIEST 911 CALLS (60 MIN.)
Hijinks ensue when emergency operators fail to respond to frantic calls for help.

THE DEEP FRIED FOOD NETWORK

7PM
NOW YOU'RE COOKING WITH GREASE! (30 MIN.)
Today: Solid waste experts give tips on disposing of used lard.

CANAL LOS STUPIDOS

7:30PM
¿QUÉ ES ESTO? (30 MIN.)
Quiz show?

COP TV

8PM
PROBABLE COZ (30 MIN.)
Worst-case situation comedy.

OMG

8:30PM
LETT3RS (30 MIN.)
FBI agents use text messaging to kill time while on a stakeout.

COP TV

9PM
SPD BLUE (60 MIN.)
Springfield's longest running police drama comes to a close when cast members become too old and flabby to do nude scenes.

CRIME TIME

10PM
CSI: SPRINGFIELD (60 MIN.)
Hijinks ensue when the chief confuses his powdered donuts with ones that were dusted for fingerprints.

NEWZZZ

11PM
KENT BROCKMAN REPORTS (30 MIN.)
Fear-mongering and celebrity gossip.

FOOX

11:30PM
THAT '90S SHOW (30 MIN.)
Hijinks ensue when a group of teenagers in Wisconsin get Rachel haircuts.

CHANNEL FLOOR

12AM
IF THIS WALL-TO-WALL CARPETING COULD TALK (60 MIN.)
Homeowner puts a house up for sale after a shampooing reveals the rug's original color.

THE REDNECK NETWORK

1AM
RANGER, TEXAS WALKER (60 MIN.)
After Ranger delivers a roundhouse kick to the villain, the shot is shown repeatedly from different angles.

CLASSIC CRAPPY MOVIES

2AM
POLICE ACADEMY XIV (2 HRS.)
Meryl Streep stars as a misfit recruit attempting to prove herself as a police officer in this critically acclaimed drama.

HOMELAND SECURITY

4AM
THE OTHER BIG BROTHER (60 MIN.)
Public restroom surveillance video outtakes.

• Anyone who detonates a nuclear device within the city limits of Chico, California, is liable to a fine of $500.

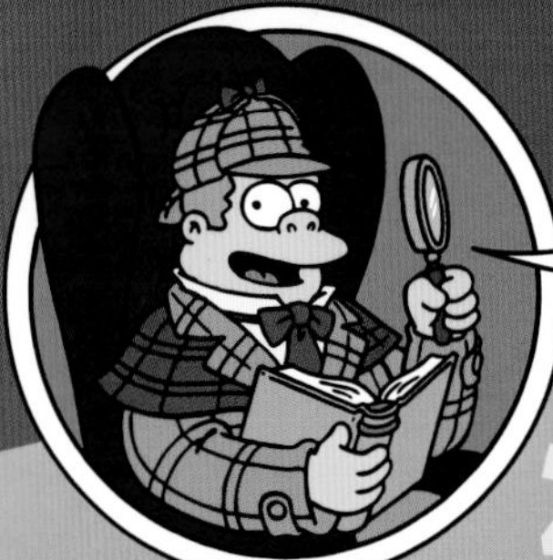

25 BOOKS TO READ BEFORE YOU'RE MURDERED

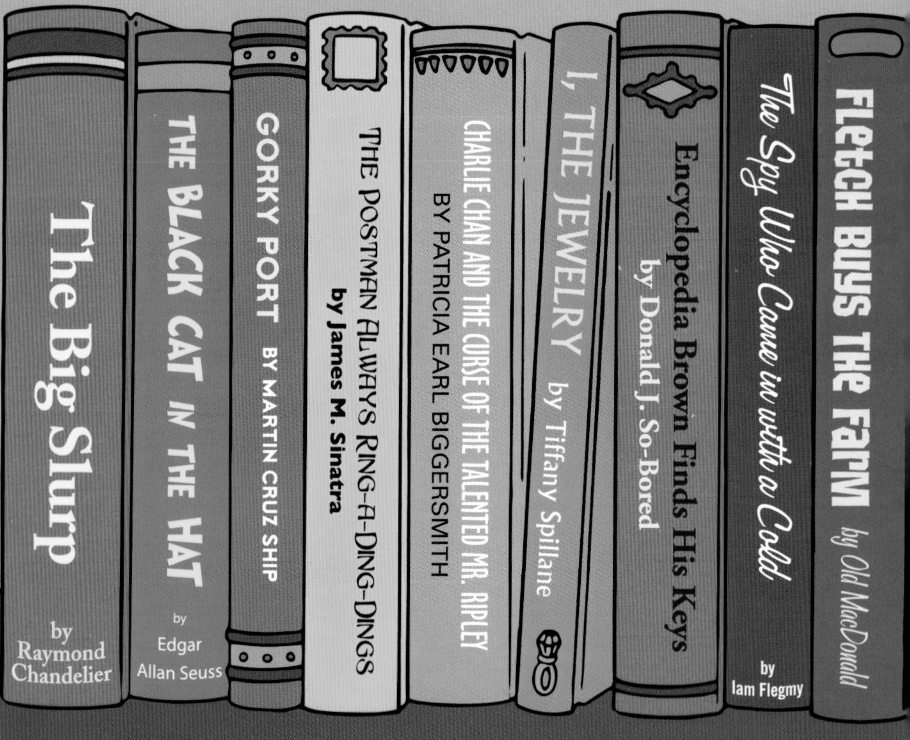

• It is illegal to take a French poodle to the opera in Chicago.

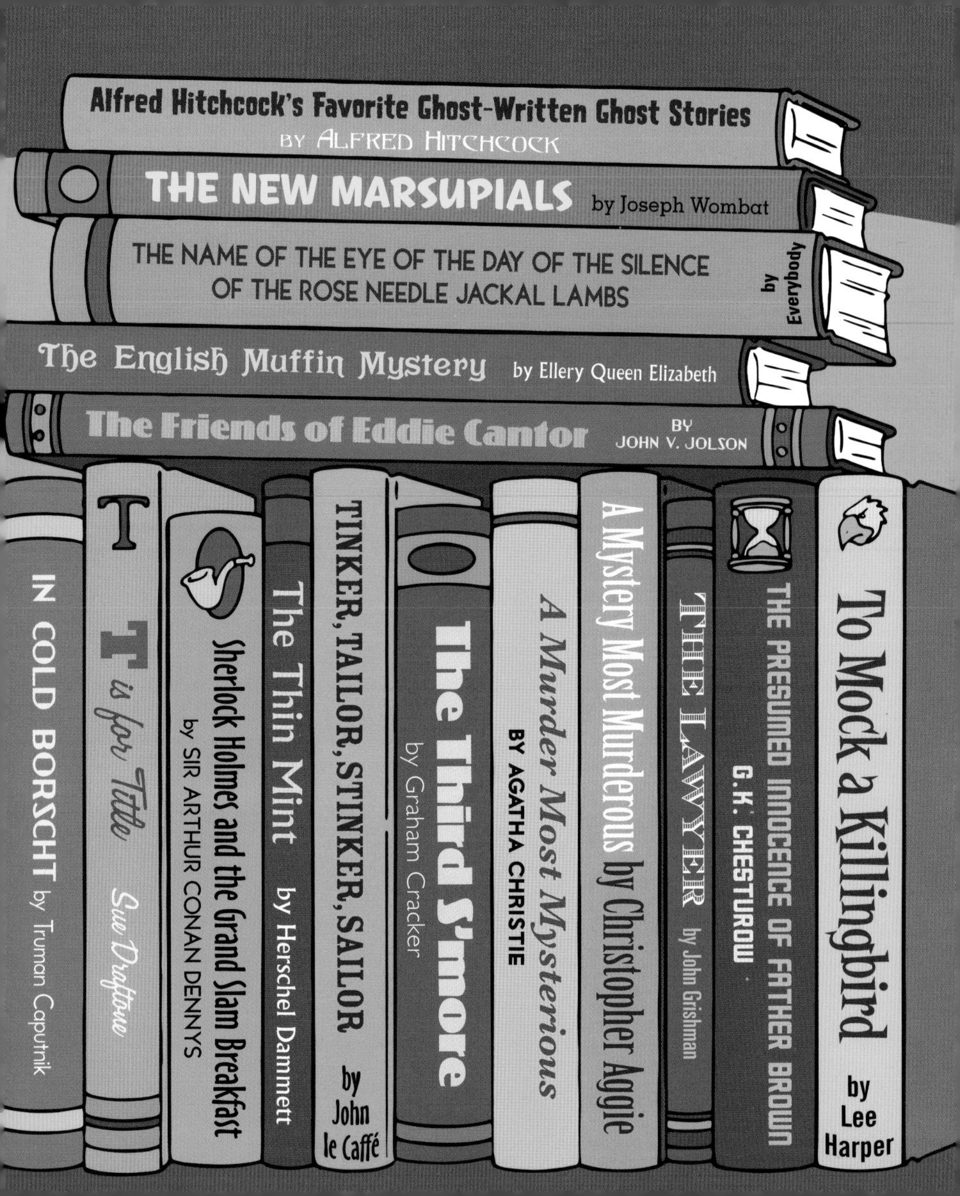

Alfred Hitchcock's Favorite Ghost-Written Ghost Stories
BY ALFRED HITCHCOCK
THE NEW MARSUPIALS
by Joseph Wombat
THE NAME OF THE EYE OF THE DAY OF THE SILENCE OF THE ROSE NEEDLE JACKAL LAMBS
by Everybody
The English Muffin Mystery
by Ellery Queen Elizabeth
The Friends of Eddie Cantor
BY JOHN V. JOLSON
IN COLD BORSCHT by Truman Caputnik
T
T is for Title
Sue Draftone
Sherlock Holmes and the Grand Slam Breakfast
by SIR ARTHUR CONAN DENNYS
The Thin Mint
by Herschel Dammett
TINKER, TAILOR, STINKER, SAILOR
by John le Caffé
The Third S'more
by Graham Cracker
A Murder Most Mysterious
BY AGATHA CHRISTIE
A Mystery Most Murderous by Christopher Aggie
THE LAWYER
by John Grishman
THE PRESUMED INNOCENCE OF FATHER BROWN
G.K. CHESTUROW
To Mock a Killingbird
by Lee Harper

BADGES! I NEED MY

CHIEF WIGGUM'S COLLECTION OF POLICE

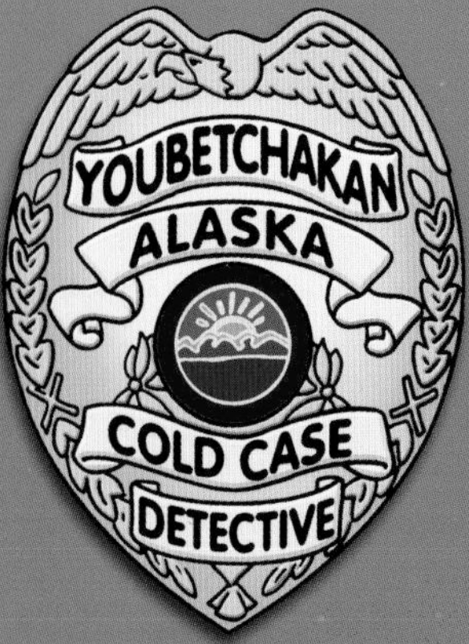
YOUBETCHAKAN
ALASKA
COLD CASE
DETECTIVE

MOTTO: FREEZE!

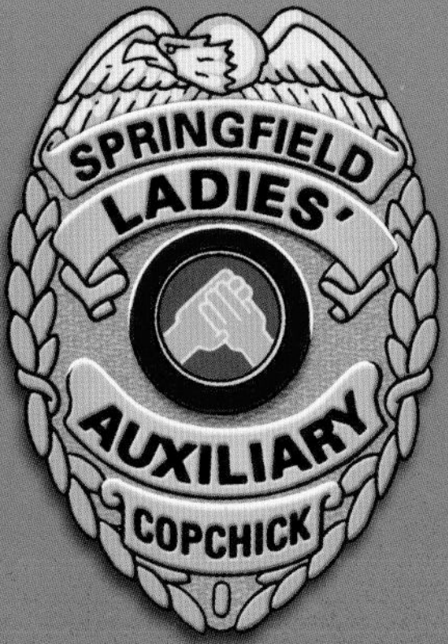
SPRINGFIELD
LADIES'
AUXILIARY
COPCHICK

MOTTO: IF YOU CAN'T STAND THE HEAT, GET OUT OF MY LINE OF FIRE!

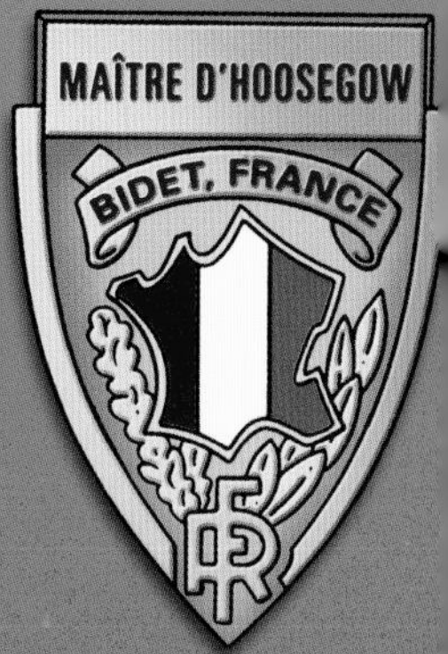
MAÎTRE D'HOOSEGOW
BIDET, FRANCE
RF

MOTTO: C'EST LA VIE!

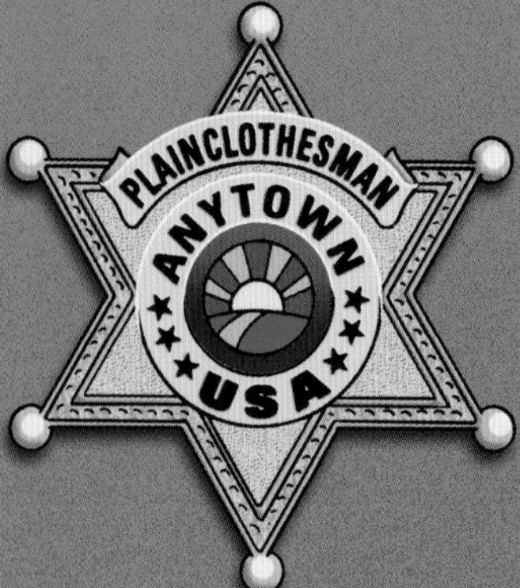
PLAINCLOTHESMAN
ANYTOWN
USA

MOTTO: MOVE ALONG. NOTHING TO SEE HERE.

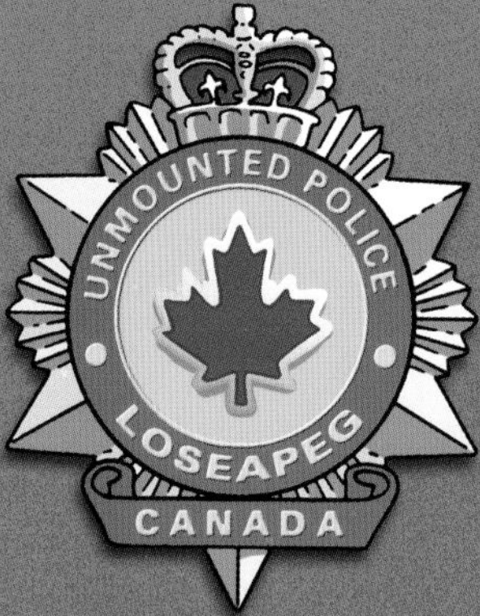
UNMOUNTED POLICE
LOSEAPEG
CANADA

MOTTO: WE ALWAYS GET OUR MANITOBA.

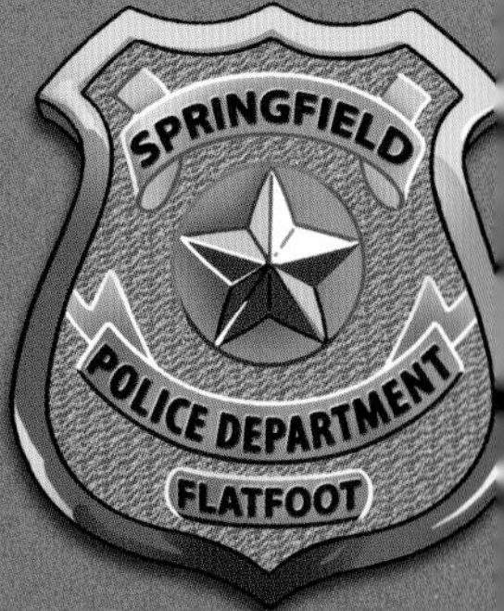
SPRINGFIELD
POLICE DEPARTMENT
FLATFOOT

MOTTO: CASH BRIBES ONLY.

STINKIN' BADGES!

BADGES FROM AROUND THE WORLD

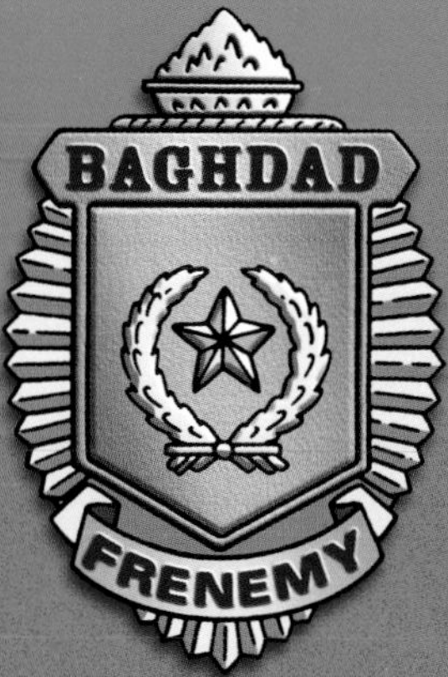
BAGHDAD
FRENEMY

MOTTO: AS YOU STEP DOWN, WE STEP ASIDE.

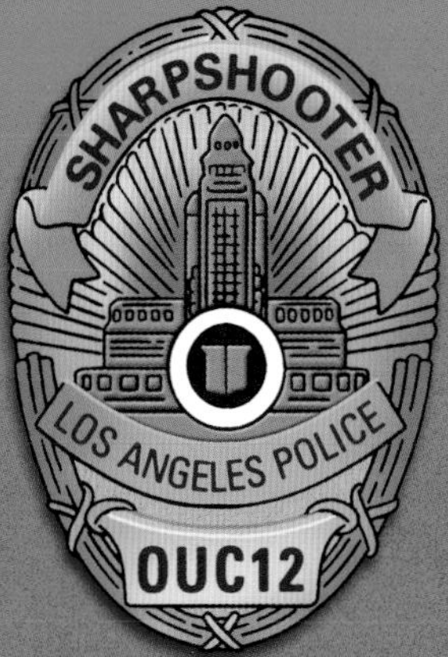
SHARPSHOOTER
LOS ANGELES POLICE
OUC12

MOTTO: TO PROTECT AND TO SERVE (JUST KIDDING).

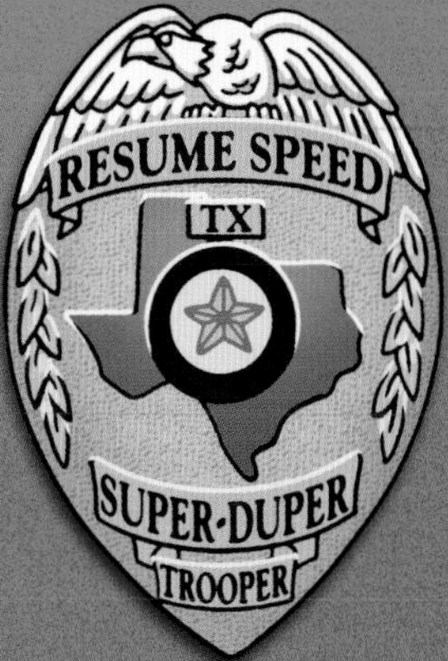
RESUME SPEED
TX
SUPER-DUPER
TROOPER

MOTTO: YEEHAW.

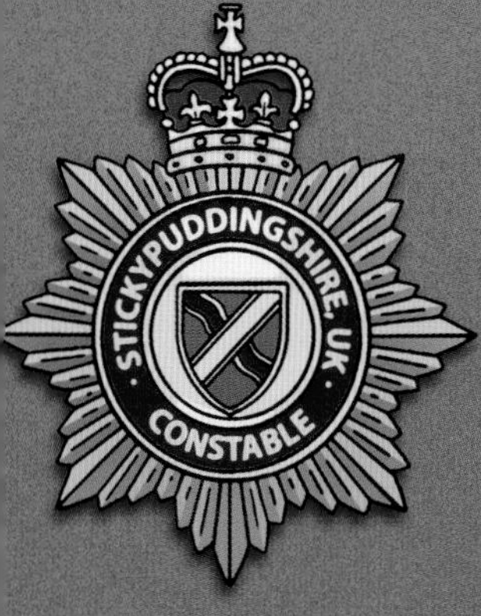
STICKYPUDDINGSHIRE, UK
CONSTABLE

MOTTO: 'ELLO! WHAT'S ALL THIS, THEN?

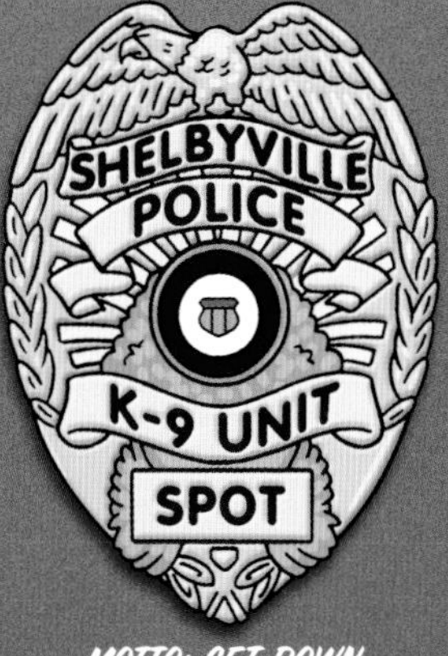
SHELBYVILLE
POLICE
K-9 UNIT
SPOT

MOTTO: GET DOWN OFF THAT SOFA!

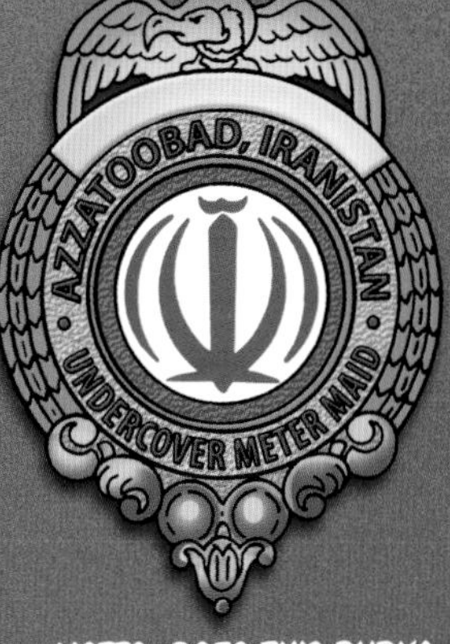
AZZATOOBAD, IRANISTAN
UNDERCOVER METER MAID

MOTTO: DOES THIS BURKA MAKE ME LOOK FAT?

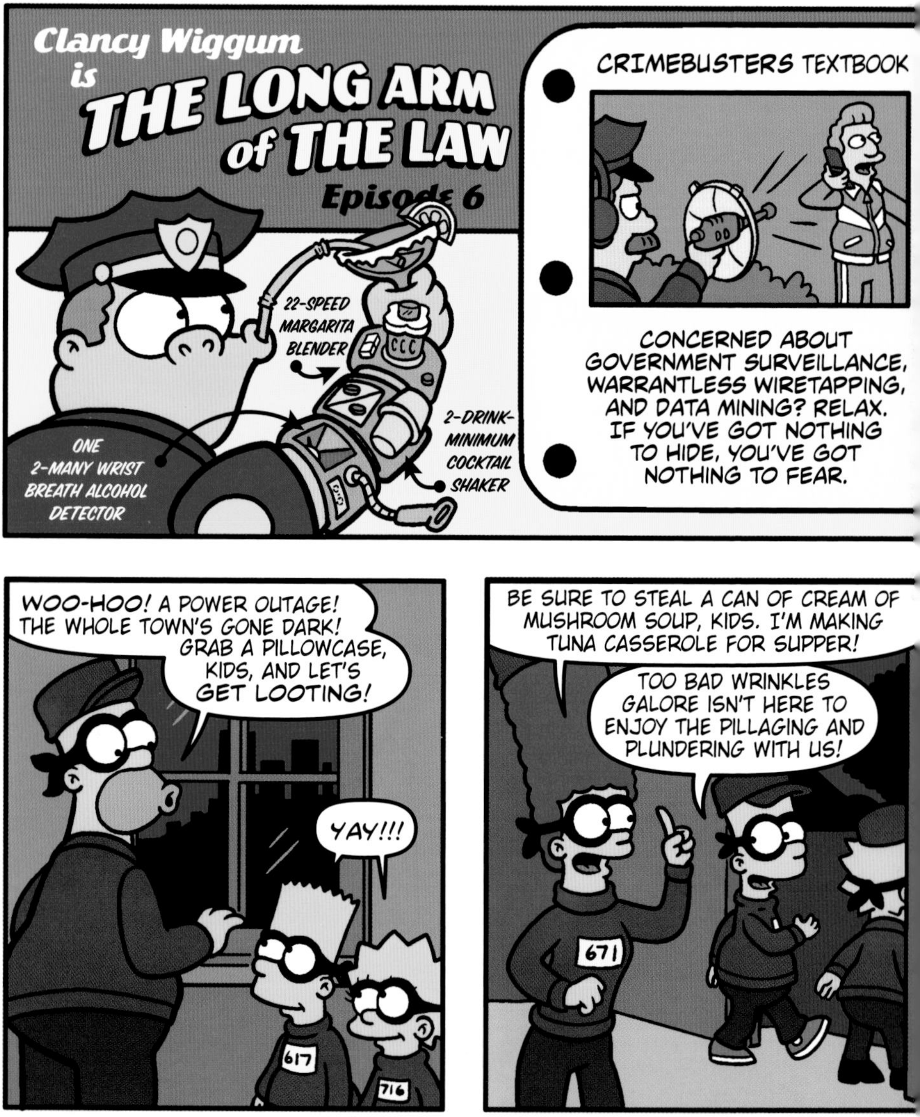
Clancy Wiggum is
THE LONG ARM of THE LAW
Episode 6
22-SPEED MARGARITA BLENDER
2-DRINK-MINIMUM COCKTAIL SHAKER
ONE 2-MANY WRIST BREATH ALCOHOL DETECTOR
CRIMEBUSTERS TEXTBOOK
CONCERNED ABOUT GOVERNMENT SURVEILLANCE, WARRANTLESS WIRETAPPING, AND DATA MINING? RELAX. IF YOU'VE GOT NOTHING TO HIDE, YOU'VE GOT NOTHING TO FEAR.
WOO-HOO! A POWER OUTAGE! THE WHOLE TOWN'S GONE DARK!
GRAB A PILLOWCASE, KIDS, AND LET'S GET LOOTING!
YAY!!!
617
716
BE SURE TO STEAL A CAN OF CREAM OF MUSHROOM SOUP, KIDS. I'M MAKING TUNA CASSEROLE FOR SUPPER!
TOO BAD WRINKLES GALORE ISN'T HERE TO ENJOY THE PILLAGING AND PLUNDERING WITH US!
671

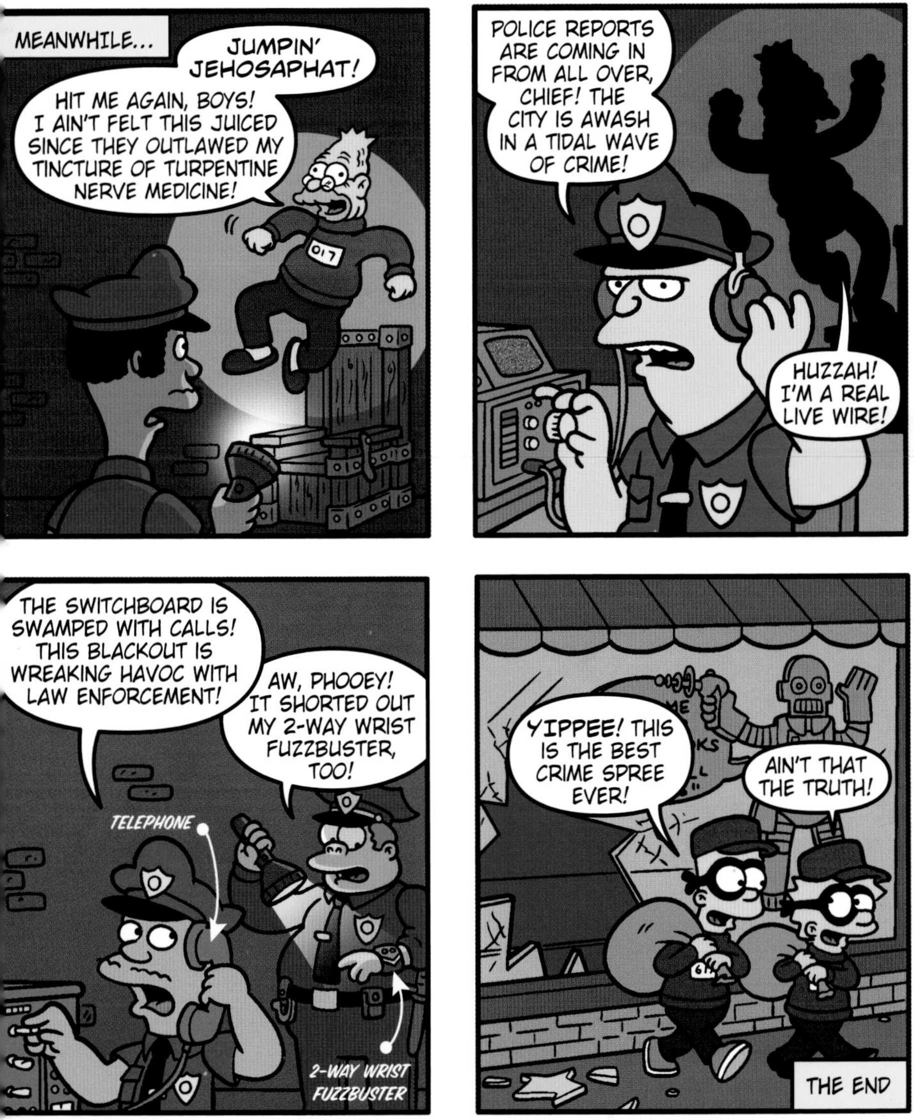
MEANWHILE...
JUMPIN' JEHOSAPHAT!
HIT ME AGAIN, BOYS! I AIN'T FELT THIS JUICED SINCE THEY OUTLAWED MY TINCTURE OF TURPENTINE NERVE MEDICINE!
017
POLICE REPORTS ARE COMING IN FROM ALL OVER, CHIEF! THE CITY IS AWASH IN A TIDAL WAVE OF CRIME!
HUZZAH! I'M A REAL LIVE WIRE!
THE SWITCHBOARD IS SWAMPED WITH CALLS! THIS BLACKOUT IS WREAKING HAVOC WITH LAW ENFORCEMENT!
AW, PHOOEY! IT SHORTED OUT MY 2-WAY WRIST FUZZBUSTER, TOO!
TELEPHONE
2-WAY WRIST FUZZBUSTER
YIPPEE! THIS IS THE BEST CRIME SPREE EVER!
AIN'T THAT THE TRUTH!
THE END

CHIEF WIGGUM'S BOTTOM 40

1. MAYOR QUIMBY.
2. ANYTHING THAT RHYMES WITH "CLANCY" OR "WIGGUM."
3. THE VILLAGE PEOPLE.
4. DIRTBAGS (AS IN CRIMINALS, NOT ACTUAL BAGS FILLED WITH DIRT).
5. CHEAPSKATE BRIBERS.
6. MEASLY MISDEMEANORS.
7. RUBBER BULLETS.
8. THE MONOTONOUS BLAH, BLAH, BLAH OF THE MIRANDA WARNING.
9. PAUSING TO RELOAD.
10. THE FOURTH AMENDMENT.
11. TEPID COFFEE.
12. CAVITY SEARCHES.
13. SUSPECTS WHO FLEE ON FOOT.
14. SO-CALLED PROBABLE CAUSE.
15. SO-CALLED INNOCENT BYSTANDERS.
16. SO-CALLED REASONABLE DOUBT.
17. SO-CALLED COMMON LAW.
18. SO-CALLED DEADLY FORCE.

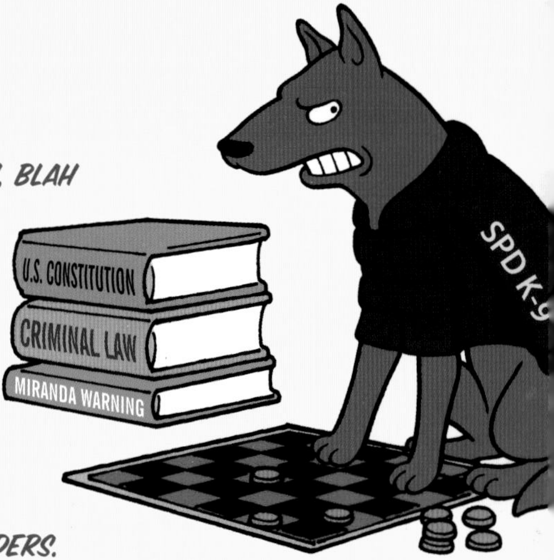
U.S. CONSTITUTION
CRIMINAL LAW
MIRANDA WARNING
SPD K-9

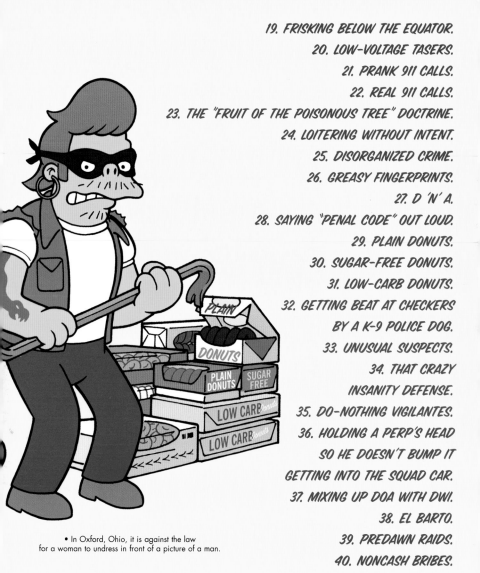

19. FRISKING BELOW THE EQUATOR.

20. LOW-VOLTAGE TASERS.

21. PRANK 911 CALLS.

22. REAL 911 CALLS.

23. THE "FRUIT OF THE POISONOUS TREE" DOCTRINE.

24. LOITERING WITHOUT INTENT.

25. DISORGANIZED CRIME.

26. GREASY FINGERPRINTS.

27. D 'N' A.

28. SAYING "PENAL CODE" OUT LOUD.

29. PLAIN DONUTS.

30. SUGAR-FREE DONUTS.

31. LOW-CARB DONUTS.

32. GETTING BEAT AT CHECKERS BY A K-9 POLICE DOG.

33. UNUSUAL SUSPECTS.

34. THAT CRAZY INSANITY DEFENSE.

35. DO-NOTHING VIGILANTES.

36. HOLDING A PERP'S HEAD SO HE DOESN'T BUMP IT GETTING INTO THE SQUAD CAR.

37. MIXING UP DOA WITH DWI.

38. EL BARTO.

39. PREDAWN RAIDS.

40. NONCASH BRIBES.

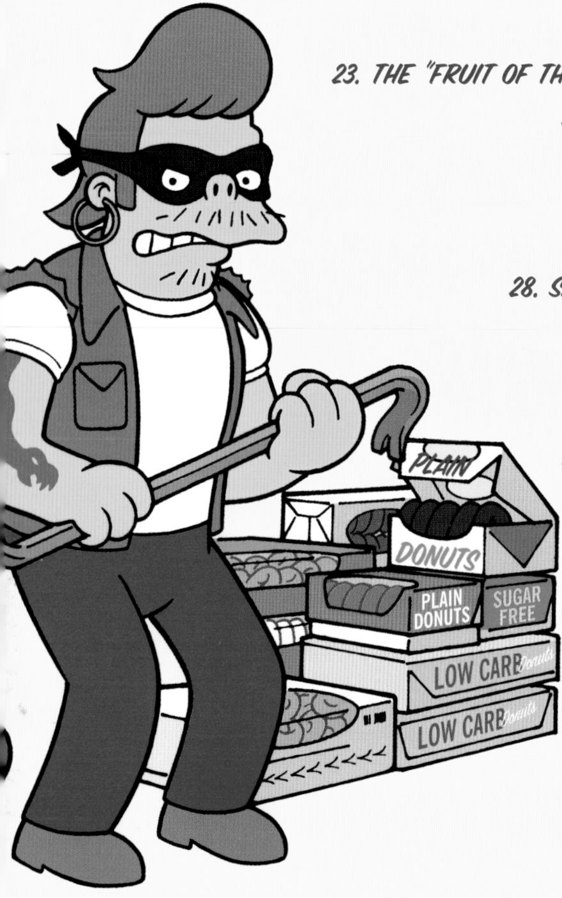
PLAIN
DONUTS
PLAIN DONUTS
SUGAR FREE
LOW CARB Donuts
LOW CARB Donuts

• In Oxford, Ohio, it is against the law for a woman to undress in front of a picture of a man.

NOW AT A NEWSSTAND NEAR YOU.

PICK ONE UP WITHOUT BOTHERING TO PAY FOR IT TODAY!

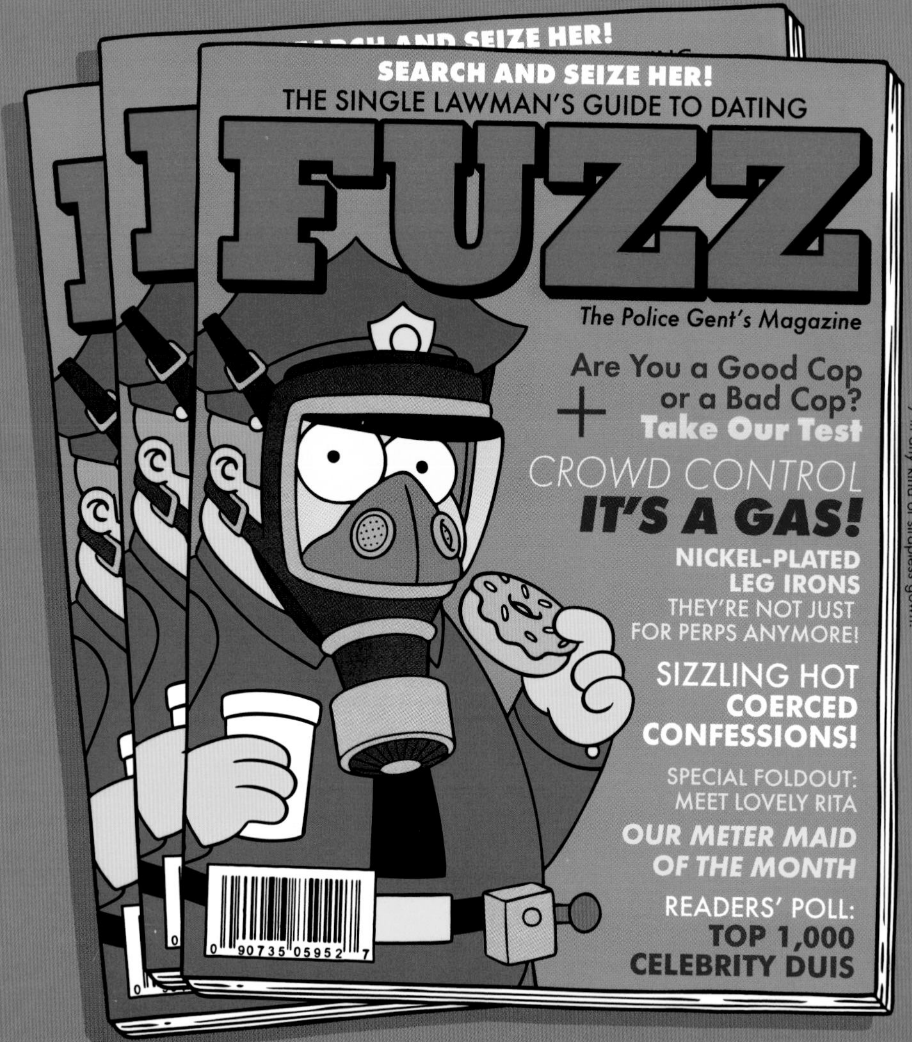

SEARCH AND SEIZE HER!
THE SINGLE LAWMAN'S GUIDE TO DATING
FUZZ
The Police Gent's Magazine
Are You a Good Cop or a Bad Cop?
+ Take Our Test
CROWD CONTROL
IT'S A GAS!
NICKEL-PLATED LEG IRONS
THEY'RE NOT JUST FOR PERPS ANYMORE!
SIZZLING HOT COERCED CONFESSIONS!
SPECIAL FOLDOUT: MEET LOVELY RITA
OUR METER MAID OF THE MONTH
READERS' POLL:
TOP 1,000 CELEBRITY DUIS
0 90735 05952 7

• Men in Florida may not be seen publicly in any kind of strapless gown.

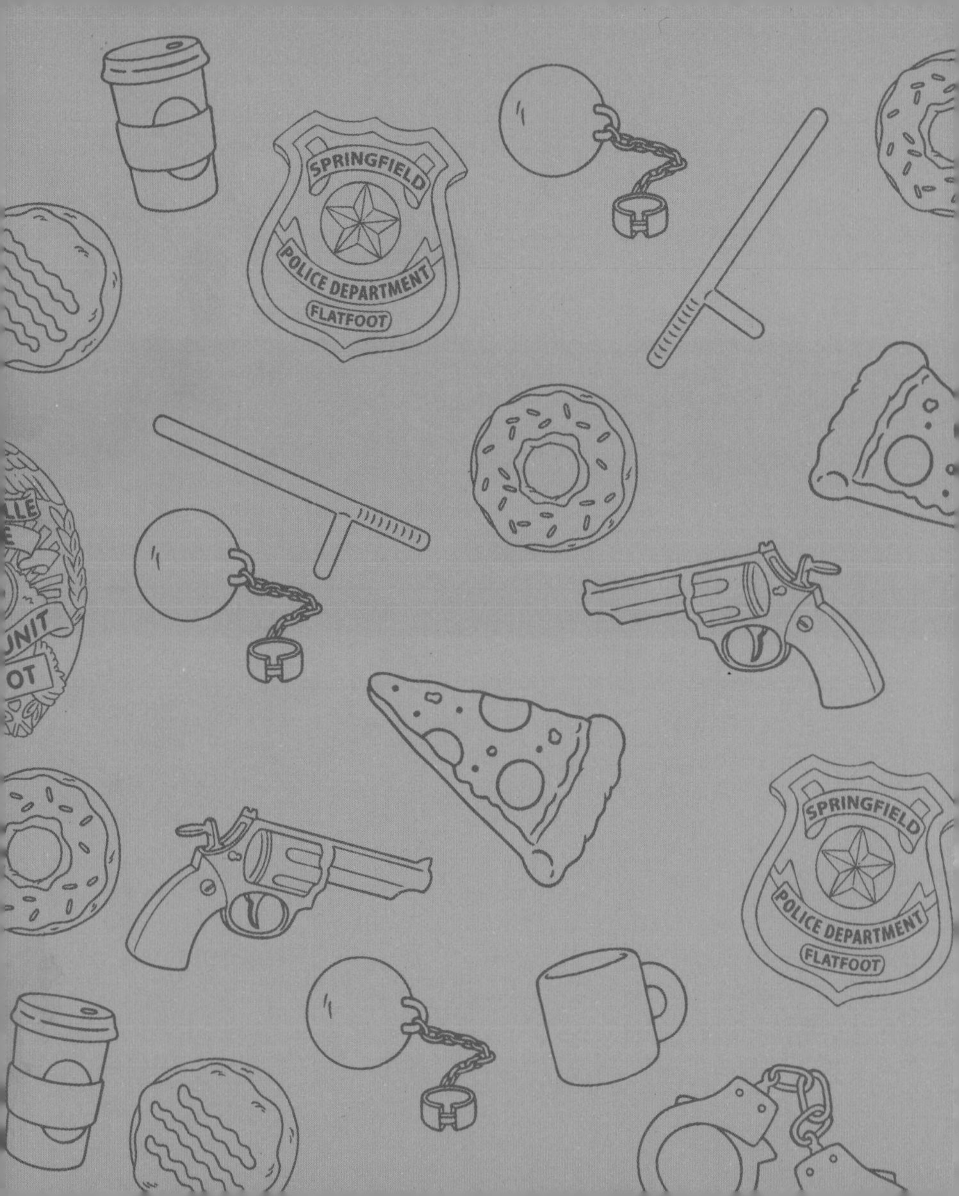
SPRINGFIELD
POLICE DEPARTMENT
FLATFOOT
SPRINGFIELD
POLICE DEPARTMENT
FLATFOOT